IN A WORLD
WE NEVER
MADE

In a World We Never Made

WE NEVER Made

A Scholarly Novel

DANIEL HILL ZAFREN

BeardBooks
Washington, D.C.

For my wonderful daughters –

Merritt, my steady light,

and Bethney, my gleaming rainbow

I, a stranger and afraid
In a world I never made.
A.E. HOUSMAN

ONE

In 1974, Blantyre University, a picturesque New Hampshire college, was often described as a spiritual replica of the University of California at Berkeley, an Eastern counterpart, even though much smaller in size. Radical writing could be traced to former students and faculty, and the spirit of intellectual rebellion still seemed to be inherent in its present teaching and student bodies. In fact, several of the faculty members were former leaders in the campus uprisings of the 60's.

It was in this setting that Justin Post hoped to recapture the past, general and personal, and to meld it into an understandable whole with societal and individual rewards. A demanding prospect for a man of twenty-eight. Yet, he would be satisfied with no less.

Admittedly, Justin Post was a dreamer. A perpetual dreamer. He suffered from that debilitating malady – inevitable and unenviable self-delusion. A fervent supporter of the inward, protective life-view. Trapped in the inexplicable dichotomy of things that never seem to change and those that never appear to be the same. Yet, as time passes all things do change. Change is deceptive, often carrying us beyond our will to points in our life's journey that we have never known before. With a person at the mercy of time and change, little wonder that reality becomes harder to find and less meaningful to hold. The present becomes inane, and a dreamer is born. The dream carries us on in the swift current of time, and we become oblivious to the subtle changes around us. Emerson said it best. *Dream delivers us to dream, and there is no end to illusion.*

Justin Post also conceded that he was also the classical case of an introvert. Yet, that had always been his strength. The ability to withdraw into himself, needing no one but himself. The impregnable inner sanctuary. That is reason enough for him to have become a writer. Even when there is an easy choice or opportunity to be an active participant in an actual event with a high degree of probability for instant and overt gratification, he would much rather write about it. The luxury and reward of being able to languish over all of the components and ramifications in true introvertish fashion. If the direction or tact is displeasing, it is possible to change it or to start over without anyone knowing about it. The partaking in a way without the actual doing, avoiding hurting others and damaging oneself. The human adventure of speculation with minimal risk.

Catching in prose any frame of time had been the outstanding and sustaining feature of his life. Little did he know that it would be such a successful aspect as well. If he had for a moment anticipated that it would have led to that kind of reality or produced that kind of practicality, it probably would never have happened that way. Even a dreamer has some limits. The boundaries of illusion are self-imposed.

While his fellow college students actively participated in the college campus upheavals of the sixties, he was busy chronologizing the events, noting the leaders, analyzing the victories and defeats, recording the impressions, and depicting the despair. He had made a systematic study of the underground press as well as a detailed diagnosis of the formation and expiration of youth movements and aspirations.

The book, *The Disestablishmentarians*, started with the earlier civil rights movements and the anti-nuclear groups. It then traced and brought to life the entire anti-Vietnam war sentiment and the events fueling discontent and agitation. It covered the formation of the Students for a Democratic Society in 1960, the assassination of President Kennedy in 1963, and the free speech movement in Berkeley in 1964. The reader felt part of the first anti-war demonstration at the University of Michigan in 1965 and the march on Washington in that same year. The major developments of 1968 thrust the reader into the frenzy of that year – the assassination of Martin Luther King, Jr.; the run by Senator McCarthy for President on an anti-war platform; the student take-over of Columbia University; the assassination of Robert Kennedy; the riots at the Democratic National Convention in Chicago; and the massive student and worker strikes in Paris. Published in October 1970, it was among the first writings to search for the deeper meaning of the killing of the students by the national guard at Kent State University. A whole chapter was devoted to the My Lai massacre and its cover-up, as well as delving into the subject of war crimes. Before going to press, the recommendations of the Special Committee on Campus Tensions, American Council on Education were published. The book dissected the weakness of that effort. While the recommendations appeared reasonable on a first reading, they lacked genuine substance. As an example, it recommended that colleges and universities must be centers for free inquiry. *[G]reat weight should be given to educating young people to realize more fully their potentials on their own terms, and to help them find new solutions to the urgent social problems of our times.* Justin had preferred and urged the more pointed solution found in one of the many published papers accompanying the report, papers none of which were written by current students. *What we really need is sustained, in-depth communication between old and young over survival questions: 1. How do we reconstruct our society to make it serve truly human purposes? 2. How do we provide the best education for preparing people to bring about that more humane society? 3. How does an individual search out and affirm personal values and purposes to guide him in acquiring his education and in taking up a creative and constructive role in society?*

The study captured the essence of the emotional, social, and political period. It had become a literary best seller, somewhat remarkable for a work of nonfiction by an unknown writer. One kind reviewer described it as an "artistic masterpiece of and for our times." It had become an annotated version of that period in history for the elders of society. It was considered as a form of diary for all of those who had participated in the events or who had been sympathetic observers. Its nature and substance took hold as a kinky, underground manifesto for the next generation entering that analogous period of restless youth. With rising sales, increased printings, and a steady flow of royalties, he was immersed in the lap of literary luxury. A dreamer, however, never turns off the spigot of imagery, and a writing dreamer never abandons the pen-filled descriptions of those illucidations.

Now that he had seen it, felt it, and described what the events were and what they meant for those involved and for society at a given time, his compulsion was to incorporate the important lessons of that period in a book. To be based in a radical college setting, and focusing on the inner activity and thinking of young minds, the fictional account and the imaginary players would hopefully help breach the canyon of despair and misunderstanding between the generations.   All with the desired end of promoting further understanding and to inspire the search for positive ends. The premise being that there are common problems that face young people in a timeless and endless fashion.   No matter how the surroundings may change, no matter how technology may give us mastery over our every day lives, the essence of the questions and search remain the same. An Arabian proverb casts it this way: *Youth is a kind of illness cured only by the passing years.*

Even as a boy, he loved proverbs. There is a form of magic in those succinct words of wisdom. A wisdom of many yesterdays, found in and crossing many diverse cultures, usually attributable to no particular individual and bearing merely a national designation. A natural guidepost for future living. Ideas to ponder over. Words to live by.

Proverbs are jewels that on the stretched forefinger of all time sparkle forever [Alfred Tennyson].
Proverbs are the literature of reason [R.W. Emerson].
Proverbs are the daughters of experience [Rwanda].
Proverbs are the wisdom of the ages [Germany].
Proverbs bear age and he who would do well may view himself in them as in a looking glass [Italy].

Justin could not and will not accept the indifference in all of his surroundings. Everywhere that he looks, everywhere that he turns, he sees and senses the non-committal, the non-action, and the non-living. He will not succumb to this modern malady no matter how much the pressures and temptations might push him in that direction.

The problem is not that he feels and thinks this way, but just how much he should try to influence others to think in such an unpopular way. Would the writing of this book be of some help or merely prove to be another hindrance in life and prompt more futile efforts at living? When self-delusion is shattered, what will rush in to take its place? Not many people are stable enough either in mind or spirit to live in a hiatus. For the mind, there is no refuge from doubt and for the spirit there is no shelter from despair. Who is strong enough to want to cast away the button-pushing for the arduous step-by-step process of original creation and production? Who wants to put aside a ready-made world to venture out on one's own? Who wants anything other than what the ever-constricting world decrees in the list of approved wants? Beyond each question lurks another one. To tackle the first means to agonizingly undertake an infinite mental journey.

For him, the dream-maker, an additional rather selfish motive. These were the same seething questions he faced. The same doubts, fears and hopes that he may have mused himself through but for which he still was not sure that he had found any lasting solutions. The momentous and puzzling problem had always been himself. In his own quest for identity, each apparent solution brought a new problem to the forefront, and he was never totally free from mental frustration and the symptoms inherent in that youthful mind pollution. This, in the guise of love, even made him shut out those that he had loved. Yet, this concept of self he considered an essential aspect of his being. It kept his mind attentive and ready to question all that appeared without logic or reason. Although there would probably always be manifestations that he could not fully comprehend, at the very least he would be cognizant of them.

The growth of his own principles had been slow and arduous, and probably would have remained undistinguished except for the torment it caused him. Being an avid reader had made him a shrewd observer. He saw a world without vision, without feeling, without shame, without mercy. Novel ideas often ignored or dismissed. People aging long before they needed to. The sense of uselessness when talents and experiences are no longer needed or wanted. Nations being far too quick to resort to hostile actions over archaic notions, or over no principles at all. False or concocted perceptions becoming an ugly reality. Unreasoning inhumanity festering beyond practical control. An aberration, or a signpost?

He hears the discordant noise of wasted energy and the stench of human corruption fills his nostrils. The dignity of people obliterated by their own fetishes, particularly those of possession and consumption. A take-all, give nothing in return, world. The misguided young, as well as the abused aged. An indifferent, traumatized society. He always knew that he could make his own world apart from most of this infliction, but he could not prevent the constant repulsion that he felt upon seeing it or even just knowing that it is there. He cannot truly rest being aware of its existence and not doing anything about it, no matter how small the contribution might turn out to be.

So, he became a sideline, writing radical in the college days of the 60's. Travelling the road from nowhere to no place. Attempting to tie isolated events into a coherent whole. Interestingly, the New Left did not begin as an activist movement. It started in academic publications, such as *Studies on the Left*, which was put out by graduate students discovering and discussing a new interest in Marxism. The direct action techniques were taken over later from the Negro movement in the South. His own so-called radicalism had developed over time into a modified Humanism, perhaps most closely described by Erik H. Erikson, as a Humanist in the sense of political, social and economic recovery with new implications. Man still as the measure, but a man far grimmer and with less temptation to congratulate himself on his exalted position in the universe. More directly, a *World Humanist* who focuses not on the concept that every person is an island but on broad humanitarian concepts and considerations. Each and every decision or course of action a person makes or takes should be based on the widest conceivable range of human possibilities.

He wanted to be at the forefront of what Allen Ginsberg has termed the *youth seekers*. He wanted to adopt the vision of the Spanish poet who wrote about there being no path for travelers but that paths are made by walking. He took faith in the credo espoused by Hesse: *The only duty we acknowledged was that each one of us should become so completely himself, so utterly faithful to the seed which Nature planted within him, that in living out its growth he could be surprised by nothing unknown to come* Or, the courage in the words of e.e. cummings: *to be nobody – but – yourself in a world which is doing its best, night and day to make you everybody else – means to fight the hardest battle which any human being can fight; and never stop fighting.*

What kind of book could he write that might convey such insight, knowledge and direction? It cannot work miracles. It cannot relieve the pain of growing or cushion the trauma of living. Knowledge is a vibrant absorption, and it takes people who love it, who are dedicated to it to impart its intricate beauties, its most subtle challenges. It matches in multiplicity all of the quirks of human machinations. The involvement in and mastering of differences. Comparison is useless without standards, standards impossible without testing, testing lacking without thought, and thought empty without reason. We live in endless circles, each crossing other lives, other thoughts, at random points on the circumference. Even knowledge is an endless and beginingless circle. Perhaps, the greatest circle of them all. It has to be to touch all of us, to allow each one of us to participate in its movement. People must come to the realization that it can be one of the strongest bonds joining all humanity, The rights to life, health, knowledge, and happiness. The ultimate human rights. A boundless enterprise. Room for theory, experimentation, and establishment. A limitless journey of intellect. Too vast for one person to comprehend and master, too challenging for one not to try.

Why not pose questions even if no answers are apparent? Why not diagnose, dissect, and analyze all of the sensitive and baffling complexities of various ideas? It is to that pursuit, to that attempt to meet the daring challenges, that he will dedicate his energies in writing this new book. A lofty motive for a dreamer's ramblings. Yet, his dreams would not be stilled. Their pulsation absorbs him, inviting him to dwell in his inner thoughts and feelings. At the same time, they eject him out into the universe, beyond himself and into all of the mysteries that humanity can aspire to. Worlds to explore and exploit.

TWO

It had been relatively easy for Justin Post to obtain a teaching position at Blantyre University, particularly with his credentials, as well as his well-known publication. He was to lead a seminar entitled "Modern Anarchism." It seemed like a perfect backdrop and impetus for his new book.

The seminar, described in the school catalogue as involving the *exploration and communication of novel and radical ideas based on past Anarchist teachings,* was general enough for him to use his past research as a foundation. As he was told, the most active members of the student body would be registered for this seminar. This, he hoped, would work to his advantage. It also would let him be a member of the Political Science Department, in which most of the radical faculty members were ensconced, many of them of long-standing duration. Some of the names, and many of their writings, had appeared in his original study. Ideas etched in the philosophy of adamancy.

Staring out of the window of the small office that would be his scholarly retreat, the expansive tree-lined campus stood out in bold beauty in the crisp September air. Within the next few days it would be cluttered with the returning students, and the now tranquil setting would be seething with anxious activity. His increasing exhilaration at the prospects that lay before him made it difficult to concentrate on the details of his pursuits. He knew that things would not be simple after this. Unwittingly, his eyes closed. Images drifted across the barren spans of his mind, mere wisps to gaze upon but which cannot be held. A young woman running across a field. Her breath sending out a cloud vapor into the winter air, a long pony tail dangling beneath a red wool hat and swinging as she ran. She was running to him and into his arms, clutching him with such feeling that it reflected a concept little understood, especially by him at the time, that the power of human emotion is virtually limitless. Looking down into the clear blue eyes, the frail body exuding a power of form and content even though the coat concealed its most feminine formations. Feeling the warm full lips against his chilled cheek, and hearing her repeat over and over again in a sensuous whisper, "I love you........I love you."

That ardent look and comforting voice were still as real and familiar as if it had occurred the minute before rather than the years since its actual transpiring. Years and many emotions dissipated since what should have been a life-long moment. Why couldn't he have realized what he had at the time and striven to perpetuate it rather than to destroy it? That is what he had done. Not really intentionally, but that mattered little in hindsight. Nor did it soothe the ravages of his guilty conscience about what had happened not only in what he had probably done to her but also what he abandoned in the process. He had smothered the very essence of a beautiful, living passion, a sincere form of life that had its own freshness and vibrancy. Perhaps, only once is a love like that experienced by any person – if ever. That is what it had been. It had begun that way, and would have continued for a human eternity if he had not subjected it to self-imposed stresses that it could not withstand. Contrary to popular thinking, love itself is not endless strength. It is vulnerable to destruction from within.

It had all started when he met Rosalind. It had been a romantic encounter, one that would probably have stirred the fire in any young heart. They had met first at a civil rights march in Washington arranged by the college activist group. On the return bus ride that evening, they sat together and talked for hours. Sharing the intricate workings of their minds and hearts. So much to talk about, and yet it barely had been the scratching of the surface to many profound treasures. Numerous and lengthy discussions ensued, and emotional involvement was deep and earnest. Parallel reactions and sensations. They became inseparable as if fictional lovers in their own book of life. That same evening when she let her head rest on his shoulder, he had never felt a greater contentment. Long after the others had gone to sleep, their hands clasped in the silence that surrounded them. Even that silence seemed to communicate a distinct meaning, a secret that true lovers only know.

The first time that he kissed her was still sharp in his memory. It was such a warm and tender kiss that he trembled with its composite of strength and fragility. The salt from her tears was fresh on his lips. "We fit together so nicely," she murmured in his ear. He held her close, and for that moment the world was a perfect place, the cosmos inviting and exciting to the living spirit. In that instant, knowing but without learning it, he had experienced the best that life can offer.

> *Experience is not always the kindest of teachers,*
> *but it surely is the best* [France].

Yes, that had been a wonderful beginning for the ecstatic dreams sheltered within his breast. It had been the burning source for his most sensitive insights, enabling him to write with a flowing pen. But, he had not been ready for what then had portended to be its monumental consequences. One must be primed in order to cope with an orderly transition from dreams to reality. He was not prepared, not capable of accepting it or to believe that it was really happening. Too many other things preoccupied his thoughts and attention. His blatant lack of maturity enabled distractions to carry him away. His priorities and perceptions were then far from clear, adding to his own personal transformation in the aging process. Attributable solely to his own weaknesses, he failed to recognize or even accept that the simplest things of life can be the sweetest and the most enduring. His immaturity prevailed over what he should have garnered and harvested. Totally irresponsible and probably the dumbest action of his entire life. Feeble excuses for extinguishing the flame of promise. A poor philosophy for one now claiming such worldly wisdom, and who wishes to become a guru.

Now that he was at the point in his life when he felt that he could accept such a love for what it was and what it can be, a certain despair clouded his enthusiasm. Now that he could appreciate it, nourish it, it ironically eluded him. Or was it just his guilt and malcontent that impaired his sensory feelings? Not that he expected to find a replica of that earlier passion here at Blantyre. That would be too much to expect. What he was hoping to accomplish along with the general pursuit would be some assistance in analyzing his own feeble role in that personal saga. Observing people of that like age in a college setting seemed to be the proper framework for such an introspection. To dream without agitation. To find, perhaps, in the creative literary world a tiny speck of personal solace.

He had often wondered what had happened to Rosalind. Their separation had been complete and cold thanks to his shallow patience and gruff mannerism. He had heard about her once in awhile over the years right after college, and had even heard that she had married. Nothing since then to satiate his curiosity. He wished she was happy, and that the years had been kind to her recollection of his weak role in her life. Perhaps, she might remember some of those tender moments as well, noting that not every potential can be realized and that in a relationship with another person one can be totally without fault and yet the damage can be done just the same at the hands of the other. Enough damage for both. A doing of the wrong thing for all of the wrong reasons. Material and thoughts for another book. At another time. In another life.

He put his face in his cupped hands, eyes stinging. He felt so much older than his actual years, so barren of the fruit of his expectations. Not even outward success can mask that famine of the soul. Life is not an object to be taken lightly. People are not to be manipulated at our own personal whims. To live well and to be proud of doing such takes constant diligent efforts. To be careful about current actions as well as perceptive about consequences. A concern for others is one of life's most noble achievements. One slip can lead to years of heartache and remorse. Disappointment with oneself is the most difficult failure to overcome.

The conceptual fragments were dispelled by a knock at the door. He swiveled around in the chair just as Dr. Mington, the Chairman of the Political Science Department, came through the door. Dr. Mington, a short and stocky man with a thick, graying beard, proceeded to a small chair in front of the desk. He slouched down in it as if he were seeking more than just physical comfort from its structure and support. He peered deeply into the eyes of the youthful face before him. For a brief second he saw himself at a time not so long ago. It was a pleasant face, with strong and determined features. Perhaps, there would be some identification by the students with this young man. His own line of communication with them was severed and hopelessly beyond repair. But with this man, still young enough to be compassionate with their ideals and purposes, still near enough in time and space to retain a smattering of empathy, tolerance and understanding, a glimmer of hope existed. He sighed before he spoke. "Just one more week to the first class. The opening of the fervent game. What sort of vibrations are you experiencing?"

Justin took a few moments before he spoke. During all of their prior discussions, which had been quite lengthy at times to acquaint a newcomer to all that was to be expected, he had perceived that beyond an apparent surface bitterness, Dr. Mington was a disturbed man. It troubled him for he had taken an instant liking to this distinguished gentleman, and he found it increasingly difficult to curb the inquisitiveness that arose from his observations. Dr. Mington was not and had never been a radical. As probably the most conservative member of the Department, he had been its Chairman for many years. The result of compromise among the others, or as a special recognition for his numerous non-controversial treatises in the field of American Government, or both. Justin had been careful to avoid any conversation about personal lives, sticking strictly to University matters. The impulse was now more difficult to control, but he knew it was far wiser not to steer the discussion into a direction that might lead to an entrapment from which he might not be able to extricate himself diplomatically. It was not until later that he was to confirm his suspicions about how very troubled the man was, and how pitifully close he was to a personal decline.

Prudence dictated that Justin should speak first. "Working on a book and teaching are not going to be as easy as I first thought it would be. A search for some form of balance may take all of my energies."

Dr. Mington picked up on that dangling thread quickly. "Such misgivings are usually the forerunner of great undertakings, and here you are tackling two demanding tasks. It may bring out the best in you, or maybe the worst. You may be surprised, however, that the seminar may turn out to be a very challenging endeavor. With the book, you are your own antagonist. In the seminar, while experiments, theories and methods are not preordained, that seemingly boundless intellectual freedom is a proverbial two-edged sword. Young people are unpredictable. Young radicals are desperately unpredictable. Usually, the student is a veritable sheep. Occasionally, he is a jackass. Yet, once in awhile he is a lion that can devour an adversary with one fell swoop, showing not a single iota of mercy beforehand or any remorse afterwards. By design, or even by accident, they may get you into a juxtaposition. They will relish your squirming, luxuriate in your torment. Not to frighten you but to forewarn you, at that moment you will know an aloneness that you may never have experienced before. None of them will raise a finger to bring you out. You must do it all on your own. It will be a test of sorts. Your personal test. And if you do not succeed, they will exploit that vulnerability at every turn. If you prevail, that will not end the matter. Patiently, cunningly, they will set other traps for you until they determine your frailty. There will be those agonizing moments that we all have shared with our most inner selves, when we ponder deep down who is the pupil and who is the teacher. In philosophical parlance, those who are to lose, and those who are already lost. College is a strange conglomeration of societal institutions. Part courtroom, part zoo, part prison, and part an indeterminable abyss of fomenting human emotions to make Hell seem like a grand resort. I sound harsh, I know, but I have definitely become jaded in my twenty years here. I have seen it all, but understand hardly any of it. Jaded or burned out, only the label on the jar changes. I am not quite sure that at this juncture I even want to understand any of it. You are lucky that you only will have a year in this role as a mental gladiator".

Justin had listened intently, weighing the imponderables and the innuendoes. His own intellect told him that it would be wise not to carry this line of conversation any further, so he resorted to a standard dodge. When in doubt, lighten the air with a little humor, no matter how feeble the attempt. "I gather you are saying I swim or sink on my own. I only hope that when I dive in that there is enough water in the pool so that I don't bang my head, the most vulnerable part of my anatomy. The blunder wonder."

Dr. Mington seemed relieved in his own way at the casualness of the response. He chuckled. "I am not a trained life guard, but I won't be too far away if disaster and chaos reign supreme". He rose, and as if dismissing all that was said before with a wave of his hand, he exited with an intense gaze and a smile that could easily have been a sneer. Dr. Mington was indeed an interesting man. Deeply perceptive, and a true intellect. Justin admired the way that he carried his apparent agony so well. Each person has his own dark secrets, hidden away from prying eyes, inscrutable and indestructible. He recalled reading an appropriate thought, that nobody could hang a shingle outside of his home that said that there are no skeletons inside.

As for Dr. Mington, when he reached his office the world seemed to be closing in around him. He brooded in the silence that pressed around his being. A long time later, he reached for the telephone. As distasteful as the deed had become, and as much as the disgust of his own existence appeared to be swelling about him, he felt duty bound to call his wife. Long ago he had withdrawn totally into himself, and he should have known that it would have drastic and deplorable effects upon his wife and children. Yet, he ignored it until now, until it was probably too late. He had, up to this juncture, given up on his own needs, surrendered to the false security of ignoring his personal torment, and in the process had not expended the slightest effort towards fulfilling the needs or satisfying the desires of those who depended on him the most. Now, upon his discovery that he could care for someone to the outer limits of feeling, he promised himself that he would attempt to channel it in a direction that for once would be unselfish. He would make it all up to them. Even if it was the last thing that he would ever do. If only he could get her out of his mind, banish her from his heart.

Inadvertently, his glance shifted to the calendar. Two more days and she would return to the campus. No more than a mere child, an infant of man, to whom he had secretly placed in a position of worship. Caught in the spell of a terrifying source. She had no idea that he looked upon her as anything but a promising journalism student who helped him in the office to be close to any faculty discussion that she enjoyed and found stimulating. Nor would she ever know how he felt about her. Yet, he could do nothing to subdue the spark she caused within him, no matter how he tried. The separation over the summer was unbearable. Just to see her, to watch her graceful movements, to be close to the wholesome purity of her vitality. The agony of it all – to be thrust from a state of total indifference to discover anew the feeling, pulsating world. The glorious ecstasy of living. He had never sensed any reciprocal feeling in those pale blue eyes, and he guardedly maintained an appearance of aloofness. Estelle Winslow. The name rang in his ears, pounded in his chest, and the trickle of moisture that slid down his cheek only served to accentuate his turmoil. All of the years he had so easily avoided an emotional involvement with a student. Now his whole life seemed to be racing towards a collision of will and temptation. The transition was too sudden, too exciting for a man of his age. Knowing what he had not been doing all of those years was a sobering awakening. He had to use all of his energies to right it. Such a course would veer him away from Estelle, away from a rebuff, away from the forbidden fruit. No matter what, things would never be the way that they were. His life, his thoughts, his being, were consumed by an insatiable fire of desire. No longer totally the master of his mind, the paths before him were buried in smoke.

He took his hand off of the telephone. He should wait at the office longer, but he felt trapped and needed some fresh air to clear his brain. He would walk home, and wonder how long he could sustain this new outlook before he would fall as a hapless victim to the searing passion that gripped him.

As he rose, his fingers trembled slightly. Somehow he knew that his resolve and good intentions would be destroyed before he reached home. The thoughts of interest and motivation to be the husband and father that he had rarely been would turn to a mere empty gesture at the reality of the confines of his home and marriage.

THREE

Justin met Kate Henderson at the special tea for new faculty members. Actually, they had known each other by name and reputation for some years. An ardent feminist and a fervent writer, she was a radical's radical at Berkeley in the 60's. Many of her shorter pieces had appeared in the underground press, and her wonderful style and pointed commentary were evident in the many books that gushed from her torrid pen. Her basic antiestablishment philosophy seemed to grow more ardent, and her writing energy appeared undaunted even to this day. She had justified her teaching the past five years at Blantyre not as a condescension to the power of authority, but as a means of perpetuating one of the truly free thinking universities remaining in the nation. Her teachings were unrestrained, and an apt reflection of the pronouncement of Paul Goodman in *Growing Up Absurd* that there is no right education except growing up in a worthwhile world. Foremost an existentialist, her creed was philosophy's basic principle that the individual man or woman gives meaning and direction to his or her life and his or her world by means of the specific acts he or she chooses to perform.

Before he actually gazed upon her, he knew that he liked her. The respect and admiration for her flair and content had long preceded their meeting and might even have set the stage for its happening. Upon facing her, he was even more pleasantly rewarded. The pictures he had seen of her were not an adequate representation. Many men might not find her especially attractive, but he discerned a petite frame gracefully carried, a skin robust but wholesome, and a face etched with dignity. Her smile was very warm and disarming, and a slight tilt of her head as she spoke accentuated her animated tones. He concentrated on her hair, and had the distinct impression that the light glistening off the brownish waves was the dynamics of her personality radiating through the top of her head. She was, above all else, natural. Completely uninhibited, there was no denying that she was her own person. The confidence she exhibited reached to all corners of the room.

She watched him intently as he shook hands politely with those closest to him, almost silently inviting him in her direction. The dark brown eyes riveted to his as he shook her small hand, and the alluring lips parted into a broad, nearly childlike smile. "Welcome, Mr. Post, to the most fashionable group in town. All primed and ready to be plucked for your experiment. I am going to enjoy having you here more than you will relish what you may find."

Rarely at a loss for words, Justin hesitated for an instant, finding the inherent wit in her words and mannerism an unexpected bonus to her person. "If they are all fashioned after you, my work may never get done or even started."

Kate Henderson had originally thought of him as an opportunist. She had read his now famous book several times, prepared to dislike it. Yet, each time that she read it she found something soothing or bonding in it, and she was frank to admit that it had inspired her more deeply as she probed the content and intent behind the lines. She had grown to respect him not for being a fence sitter, but because he had displayed the knack of being able to stand back from it all and portray the details comprising the larger images and concepts.

Now that she met him, she cast that admiration into more personal feelings. The kind of feelings that she rarely let herself indulge in, and which she secretly wished she experienced more often. The years of fighting large battles and taking on too many controversial causes had left her drained. More and more were expected of her, and there were too many unpopular debates, and too few quiet moments and fewer and fewer meaningful rewards. This was a particularly troubling point in her life. Returning to Blantyre, she had sensed a foreboding loneliness. Having the respect of her colleagues and the students was not enough, she longed for a human closeness. An aura of doom gripped her in a cold and burdensome manner. The empty campus seemed barren and harsh, reflecting her failures during the summer when she could neither write nor coordinate her thinking. Burned out, perhaps, at the age of thirty. The night before she had even cried herself to sleep. She had not shed tears like that since she was twelve, when her father had died so suddenly. In that small apartment which she had boasted was her intellectual darkroom, everything seemed to have been crushing down on her, and the tears flowed as if a flood might be able to wash her disappointments away. Kate Henderson labeled by her contemporaries as strong and dedicated. No one who dared engage her in debate could prevail or weaken her assertions. Priding herself constantly that no situation could ever get the best of her and that time and time again she could handle anything that society could throw at her. Reserved and undauntable. Now this human contact instantly and unexplainably sealed that crack in her edifice. It offset the premonition. Once again she felt at ease, once more in control. The person she was meant to be. The individual she had to be. Echoing through her mind was the personal moral that she had so often expressed. *You cannot demand understanding. To be understood, you must yourself be understanding. To be respected, you must yourself respect. And to be loved, you must yourself love.*

Disdaining the social circulation that was probably expected of him, Justin spent the next hour busily engaged in an intellectual exchange with this fascinating woman. Her animated mannerism and apparently boundless mental energy was contagious and spellbinding. He felt extremely comfortable with her, as if they had been old friends. They were contemporaries in the truest sense of the word.

Discreetly, they left together, stopped for a cup of coffee at a small diner, and their intellectual intertwining led very naturally to a physical union. It was good for him, and he had the impression that her need was as great as his own. It was more than a mere physical act. It was a deed of acceptance. The aura of positiveness enhanced the ebullient atmosphere.

She had never made love with a man after a first meeting. Not considering herself the aggressive type or even having a daring nature concerning affairs of the heart, she had usually suppressed physical desires. In fact, she had not been close with a man like this too often, and it had been a long time since her last unsatisfying attempt. Yet, she had let herself go utterly with this man, and she was not quite sure why. The fact that she felt wonderful about it was not the intellectual approach she stood by. Yet, her mind basked in the same warmth that spread through the rest of her body. Her fragmented self-worth was sealed back together. Magically, she was transformed into two distinct personalities. The Kate of old, staunch and predictable. The other, a new Kate, adventuresome and nonchalant.

A single event or relationship can have such an effect. Proven in myriad ways, countless times. For most of us, it appears only to happen to others. And so, entranced or preoccupied in observing others we, in a self-directed abandonment, do not make the most of the opportunities that present themselves. It is, after all, always there – even if only as a possibility. The vast mystery of communications between people, especially between a man and a woman. All of the subtle nuances, all of the possible varying interpretations from the looks, the words. To read the signs. An art form as well as a scientific equation. Proving repeatedly on the sending and receiving ends the complexity, the vastness of the human element.

Many eyes go through the meadow, but few see the flowers [England].

Lying there side-by-side, flesh touching flesh, it seemed inopportune to ponder on the why and wherefore. An identical need, perhaps borne from a totally different incitement and insight, placated. A discovery or a rediscovery. For all of his avowed diagnostic abilities on human behavior in trying times, he could not and did not desire to delve into it with any close circumspection. Perhaps, he did not want to lose the enchantment of the moment, or to disturb the new dream that fired his physical and mental well being no matter how temporary it might be. Perhaps, he was creating his own safe harbor, a refuge to withdraw to from the uncertainties ahead. As large a task as it might be, he was in no frame of mind to undertake self-analysis. There would be time enough for that later. The writing of the book would be a catharsis, enough of a mind searing, analytical scalding.

For now, the most important thing for him to do seemed to be the fixing of a position, a mainstay of sorts. A common thread, ever so tenuous, to bring his writing and reality into some manageable working tandem. What more could a writer ask for? The inspiration to move, the wherewithal to grasp that movement in whatever fleeting manner or form it appeared in. He even had the rather unsettling feeling that any writing or even his own life might be composing itself or was being played out on its own. The book might be writing itself. Beyond his control. Outside of his direction. A reversal of the most uncanny sort. A book composing the author. Was he merely a ghost, to take shape and substance only upon the will of his words?

He shuddered as if a chilling wind traveled down his back, and held Kate even closer. She returned the tight embrace, believing it to be a sign of passion.

FOUR

Even though a cool early morning breeze drifted through the open window of the bedroom, Leonard Mington awoke from his restless sleep damp with perspiration. Henrietta was still asleep in the other twin bed. Her sleep seemed peaceful, and as he peered at her it was sad to realize that it had been a long time since he had looked at her carefully. It had been even longer since they had slept together in the same bed. He studied the small face that had been so much a part of his life. It had aged noticeably, and the cracks and creases in the skin were easily discernable in the early morning sunlight which filled the room. Life had not been easy for her, and he had made things more difficult. No matter what hardship or trial she faced, she had to do so alone. He had been of no assistance or comfort to her.

Their eldest daughter, Suzie, had left earlier in the week for her freshman year at a small college some seventy miles away. Just far enough so that she would have to stay at the dormitory during the week and yet could come home on the weekend, if she wished. There was little in this house to entice her to come home, and he knew that she would not come home too often. If she did, the incentive would be to be with her mother and her sister. The children had been Henrietta's major life involvement, and although he was aware of the drastic alteration she was trying to adjust to, he could not bring himself to ease the way for her.

Plans had been made initially for Suzie to attend Blantyre, but he had decided she would be better off at a smaller school. Really, however, he did not want her to see things about him, and he did not want an on-the-spot reminder of his domestic failures and weaknesses. He had shirked his paternal duty with her, and had purposely avoided any close contact or discussion recently. When Henrietta asked him to speak to her the night before she left about the pitfalls of campus life and the dangers of being away from home, he had been able to successfully shrug it off by saying that if their daughter did not have principles by this time, a last minute lecture was not going to instill them in her. Thus, he was able to avoid not only forcing himself to be actively involved in his daughter's activities, but also to postpone any hypocritical projection which could only accentuate his own inane position.

Suzie was nearly the same age as Estelle, and it was depressing for him to think that the object of this new fierce attention was young enough to be his daughter. This figment of his mind was too well defined, too well nurtured, to be stymied. It threatened to destroy him, yet he was powerless to alter the course of his actions just as he was impotent to salvage any dignity from his good intentions to those around him. If he could find a way to rid himself of this self-imposed shackle, this great force that confined him, he might be able to give Henrietta the understanding and solace she needed and deserved. But the only image that arose in his mind was that of being torn asunder by a rebuff by the object of his affection, and this would further weaken him. To emerge as even less of a man.

Why hadn't she come to see him? She was back at the University. He had checked on this, but still she had not come to his office. They had arranged last June that she would continue to assist him in the office this year, and yet she had not contacted him. What drastic change had occurred during these few months to counter the one sustaining thought that engulfed him? Tomorrow was registration, and he had to see her or totally fall apart. Just to be reassured that she was as he remembered her to be. Why wouldn't his intellect control him in this situation as it did in some other ways? Why couldn't he rationally analyze his pitiful posture and sordid feelings? Was he merely an old man hungering after fleeting youth in a convenient and appealing form? Did he truly love her? Was he able to sense a sincere sentiment again, or was it solely his imagination leading him astray by letting him believe that he was human after all? Was it conscience coming to the fore to punish him in the most agonizing way possible?

Lying in bed, he felt himself repulsed by his surroundings, and out of pure selfishness he knew that he had to get out of the house just as soon as he could. He lifted himself up from the bed and headed for the bathroom while Henrietta was just beginning to stir. The bathroom door was closed, and that meant that his other daughter, Rita, had risen early and was preoccupied in the inevitable human pastime – self-indulgence.

Just as he decided to turn back to the bedroom to dress first, the door opened and she stepped out before him. Both were taken by surprise. No longer the little girl that he had remembered her to be, but a young woman. The frail body filling out, with lips at the initial stage of seductiveness. She was a sophomore in high school, and it suddenly dawned on him that this was her first day of school. He had also forgotten that along with all the other items a caring father should know. Forgotten them so that they need not be shared. He had not had a sustained serious discussion with her for many years, and its toll was obvious. The distance between them was barren and unbreachable. He had no ambition to attempt to reach out, even if it were possible.

Rita gave him a lifeless glance, and the silence and coldness said it all. There was no affection in her mannerism, no indication in the eye contact that this chance meeting was pleasurable. She stepped around him, careful that no physical contact be made.

Once in the bathroom, he dreaded having to look at himself in the mirror. It takes only an instant for all of the events to swell up and come crashing down. In only a second a lifetime of guilt can rush in, overtake you, and mercilessly submerge you in its drowning pool. This was what he was reduced to. He knew that what he was doing was wrong, that it was selfish, contrary to all reason, and in defiance of sound logic. Yet, he wanted to do it. He hated himself for it, but he could not reverse direction. A lone mortal on the beach of existence screaming to the tide not to come in. Not one soul to hear him, not an infinitesimal chance of succeeding.

By the time that he had dressed, Henrietta had breakfast on the table. Rita reached the table at the same time that he did, and after some polite good mornings, they sat down to eat. They had not eaten breakfast like this for weeks, but there was still an obvious lack of conversation. They ate in strained silence. For his part, he knew, or at least sensed, that they were hoping he would say something or show some sort of animation or give some gesture that might reassure them that in spite of everything they were still a family, a unit with existence and meaning. But as much as awareness told him what was needed, he could not bring himself to say or do anything. The tension was invincible. The love of flesh and blood was gone. He could be full of contempt for himself, loathe himself, and call himself all of the lowly phrases which would be so appropriate for the situation, but this would not change the moment or its significance. The saddest part of it all was that Henrietta and Rita knew it as well. Their eyes would glance in his direction and then drop to the table. Henrietta drew her frayed housecoat closer around her as though an uninhibited chill had set into the kitchen. He did not really belong there, and it was tragic to realize that he never did and never would.

As Dr. Mington closed the front door of his home, he felt as if he had been through a grueling ordeal. A tremendous weight had been mercifully lifted from his shoulders, and as each step carried him further away from the house, his mind turned completely to the imagery of Estelle.

The office was empty and dismal, just as he had left it. Somehow, he had hoped to find her there, and her absence sent him adrift. He sighed with the smarting realization that things would probably not be as he had dreamed they would be, and even not as they had been. What was causing this abrupt change? Was it voluntary on her part, or did something happen that had forced her to shy away from the office? Was it his position to offer assistance in the event that she needed help? Whatever, he knew that his growing restlessness and anxiety would find no respite in speculation. One way or another, he would have to find out the cause of this action, and yet in such a natural manner that it would not reveal what was harbored within him.

Work was impossible, and he found himself staring through the slats of the venetian blind to the campus below. A few students could be seen strolling about or lolling on the grass. A few of the women looked somewhat like Estelle from a distance, but as they would approach closer to his line of vision, he felt a sense of disappointment at knowing they were not the true object of his thoughts.

Immersed totally in self-pity, he wallowed in it. A form of self-punishment that made no sense in its design or effect. It only sharpened his desire, heightened his will to make it come to pass. The lowest form of human life wanting to become a king. It was ludicrous. It was pathetic. It was, however, the only thing that mattered. A desperate man, alone and empty. Drowning in his own juices. Dead at his own hand, with but one elusive straw to clutch at.

FIVE

It was unusually quiet in the room, and as Estelle Winslow lay on the bed staring at the late afternoon shadows on the ceiling, much of the enthusiasm that she had felt upon her arrival at the school had waned. The events of the past few days weighed heavily upon her, and she was glad that as a senior she had been able to arrange having one of the scarce single rooms in the dormitory. The solitude assisted her in arranging many random thoughts, although her emotional reaction to them seemed particularly unnerving. It was almost as if she were a child again, the childhood that she had often boasted was far behind her. Frivolity supposedly replaced by the maturity of education and experience. But, it was at quiet moments such as these that she was not quite sure that she was as mature as she professed to be. In fact, if she let her intellect obliterate her delusions, there were probably more things about which she was unsure of at this moment than at any earlier time of her life.

The seed that had been planted in the last school year, that gnawing restlessness of the students, was reminiscent of an earlier decade. The need for history to repeat itself, perhaps, or the obligation to complete what history had started but that its human instruments had failed to carry through. In spite of a relatively uneventful summer, the brewing situation was now larger and stronger. Even though Blantyre was very much an academic free laboratory for experimenting young minds, and many of its teachers professed to give vent to boundless mental explorations, such was not enough for an increasing number of discontented students. This posed a dilemma for her, and it threatened to usurp her own pursuits. She had a growing cause to be wary.

Much of this consternation was attributable to Ted Amherst. For the last three years that they had been at Blantyre, she had watched him emerge as the vociferous student leader. Not that she could take any credit for that development, and she would not want to. She hung on almost as if she were a hitchhiker, looking at the sights along the way but having no authoritative voice in determining the direction or pace of the trip. She dated him almost half-heartedly. However, she had committed herself with him in the sense that he was the only one she had slept with. In a way, she regretted having submitted to him. She could not deny that she found the contact of his muscular body pleasurable, and for that reason had not terminated that aspect of their relationship. There had been no compelling reason to do otherwise. Yet, she did not like the unspoken interpretation that he gave to it. He indirectly displayed a sense of ownership over her, a subtle exercise of dominion that upset her and yet fed his ego even further. She was sure she did not love him, and as these days passed she was more and more convinced that she was totally alien to his principles. In fact, since the return trip to the school, their relationship had taken a different turn.

The impetus for this development had started just as the car was leaving the city for the long ride to Blantyre. Ted was a passenger in the front with his close friend Chester Conroy who was the driver. She was alone in the back seat, affording her the luxury in the welcome silence to let her thoughts roam at random. As they headed back to an uncertain future, she knew that her fellow passengers were doing so with trepidation. She had integral personal problems that demanded her individual attention. They, on the other hand, had taken a pledge to commence confronting the college authority openly if necessary to bring about the changes they wanted. Their problems and reactions to it would be very much a public affair. She parted with them in a belief on how change should be suggested and implemented. That serious problems existed was evident. Yet, she was in favor of attempting to work out solutions from within the system itself. It seemed more credible for one to first accept the established order, and then working from that base to seek modifications rather than to disregard the existing structure and start anew. However, she could not desert these activists. She was, after all, a co-conspirator. Whether it was due to the will to identify with the struggle of youth in general or merely the bond of age, she was not quite sure, but the reason appeared unimportant in the swelling tide.

For her, extenuating circumstances existed in the strong desire to pass rapidly and effortlessly into the waves of generations that had preceded them. Her admiration for the intellect of an older man had given her an insight into the not so dissimilar aspirations of those who had traveled along the same road before. The outward appearances might be different, but like fears and hopes existed. The major revelation is that anyone at any point in time must reach a reversal from inward to outward thinking and doing. The cessation of selfish notions to enfold others in personal schemes. The sobering recognition that there are others in this world who depend not only upon your presence but also upon the strength and constancy of your support and conscience. This forces sublimation of those fears to everyday movements and feelings. For most, the day of enlightenment arrives not in the actual realization of dreams but in the cold and harsh reality of having to earn a living.

She knew that her senior year might well be the most important year so far in her young life. At the moment, she had no desire to look beyond this year. The ultimate course of her life would fall into a pattern of its own based on her discoveries and accomplishments of this period. Her family, which she had always considered the bulwark of her confidence and ability to act, would be there to guide her. However, this year she had to prove something to herself. She had to begin an analysis of the human condition, and she could find no more perfect setting than in the academic world represented by Blantyre to engage in the laborious scrutiny. Her own development was satisfactory in terms of *herself*, but there had to be more beyond that. A search for love was as close as she could express it, if she had to do so. Yet, what kind of love? Was it a love for a person, a principle, a dream, or merely the state of being able to love at all? Was it the quest for fulfillment so that she could appreciate and sympathize with the concept of emptiness? Or, if there is no such thing as complete fulfillment, was she seeking avoidance of the realm of nothingness so that whatever degree of fulfillment she reached, she might recognize it and capitalize on it?

Puzzling thoughts for a young person, and she wished that she could talk to someone about them. Her family was too close to her for an objective analysis of her being. Her friends, even the young men sitting in front of her, were too wrapped up in their own ideals and hang-ups to be of much fortifying use. Dr. Mington was the most likely person to fit such a role, but there was a strangeness about him that would inhibit her from revealing inner thoughts. She respected his intellect more than any other person she knew, but some premonition warned her that he was deeply troubled. She could not bring herself to add to his burdens. She would be unable to be totally open and frank with him. Perhaps, this was the crux of her problem, the true object of her search. In fact, it might well be the overall deep-seeded dilemma of many young people. Someone to talk to openly and honestly. Someone who will listen without being judgmental. Unhindered communication.

The voice coming from in front distracted her, and gradually she became more interested in what they were saying. Actually, only one of them was talking, although it sounded more like lecturing. Chester listened in obedient silence, his eyes fixed on the road ahead. Ted was staring at Chester's rigid profile, but he would glance back at Estelle often to make sure that she was listening. He knew that he was getting himself wound up, but it suited him. The more that he could talk, the greater the chance that he might say something brilliant and inspiring – to ignite the spark of interest and enthusiasm of his captured audience.

Ted's voice became more animated as he talked. "Energies must be concentrated on useful purposes. As a beginning, what we have to do is isolate one segment of the faculty, maybe even just one professor, to be used to develop and solidify our position. To prompt apprehension tinged with fear. The publication of the repository of power. This is going to be our opportunity to be the leaders, to dictate our terms, with firm resolve. At least in the beginning, and as far as the public is concerned, it should be thought that we are merely expressing a point of view. But, behind those iron gates, I want them to know without the slightest doubt that the world has changed. If they do not want to change along with it they will be left in the dust. The University is rightfully ours, and that is the way it has to be. Not to learn those worn-out, useless and meaningless dogmas that are classified as educational pursuits, but to branch out to new and exciting mental challenges, new horizons of meaning. To find and experiment with new truths as they unfold."

Ted paused in his rhetoric, hoping that there would be admiration for his convictions in those bright eyes. He sensed, however, that he was merely giving her the chance to mentally firm up her objection and refutation of the generalities he espoused. His appraisal was accurate. The magic of it all was escaping her, and her doubts about him as a person and about them as a couple grew larger.

He continued in a more sedate fashion. "I need not repeat for you two old friends all that I believe in. I have had a number of strategy sessions over the summer with our friends. We definitely will proceed. We will register in the anarchism seminar, to be led by Dr. Mington, and it should prove to be interesting, very interesting. He will be our pigeon. He is the darling of the faculty. His prestige and position will serve our purposes well."

Estelle wanted to retain her aloofness at this juncture, but she could feel the control over her composure and quietness waning. She could do nothing to stop the words from coming to her lips. In the instant before they were uttered, she realized that her feelings for Dr. Mington must be stronger than she had thought. "I resent dragging a fine man like Dr. Mington into the self-imposed disarray that you want to create out of the one meaningful sanity that you profess to adhere to. He is the epitome of all that is intellectual, and the pursuit of intellectualism you have stated is the salvation for youths. Probably on that point, and that one point alone, do I agree with you. Now, you want to turn this remarkable man, this learned professor, into a scapegoat, a dupe..... a ploy..... or whatever term you want to use to describe his plight. What sense does that make? He can help us by stimulating learning, and by reinforcing the reliability and predictability of intelligence. You want to revise his orientation, shatter his scholarly world so that pure emotion will prevail. He has done nothing to deserve that sort of treatment from us, and I will not participate in such a cruel action. If you persist, I will do everything I can to stop you."

For a tense moment, Ted did not answer her outburst, but she could tell that he was seething beneath that seemingly placid exterior. She had never disagreed with him so openly, had never raised her voice against anything he had said. Here she was defiantly challenging him, defying his maxims, and directly criticizing his plans. She was surprised and even delighted that such rebellion came so easily.

Ted's outward jocular mood and tone was a gallant attempt to suppress the anger he felt. It did give her an insight into a fact that he had not had the courage or will to have said to her. He loved her. "Now, listen to her! Miss high and mighty. The savior of lost souls. Mother hen protecting her chicks. Teacher's pet to the rescue. Hooray for the cavalry! What do you think of that, Ches my boy?"

Chester glanced quickly back at her, too quickly to notice that her face was flushed. "I suppose she has her opinion, and you have yours," he stammered, not daring to look at Ted.

"Nobly said ... by a coward under fire," was Ted's instant retort. "But, she is wrong, absolutely wrong. And even if she were right, her opinion must be subjugated to the worthy goals to which we are committed. It does not matter who or what is right, whatever the concept of right is anyway. We must do anything that is necessary to bring down the archaic pillars that have kept generations of young people captive to the whims and sentiments of the prudes."

Her voice was not as steady as she would have liked it to be. "Discount my opinion all you want. I will register for that seminar, but not for the reasons you have in mind. I will fight you all the way, if I have to. I just will not tolerate the destruction of a man like that."

"Listen, Estelle," Ted said in the most mellow voice he was capable of, obviously trying to placate her, "Dr. Mington is not going to be destroyed, or anyone else for that matter. The balance of opportunity is on our side, and we must take advantage of it. We are not doing it just for ourselves, but to liberate all of the young people who follow after us. Dr. Mington will serve us as a test, a mental foil to parry with and to disarm as a warrior of the state. It will be a skirmish to solidify our stance. But nothing will happen to him. I promise you that. His intellect will be put to the supreme test, and he may even be able to overcome us with astute reasoning, but I doubt it. Yet, we will give him that chance. And that's more than he or the rest of the whole rotten world would ever give us."

Attempting to be calm, she spoke as slowly as she could sensing that this might be the last chance for her to make her arguments heard and listened to. "We all realize that things have to change. But, there are no remedies we can say for sure are better than the evil to which they are directed. I am not sure in my own mind about the means that should be used to bring about those changes. It is dangerously reckless to assume that we have the answers. One thing is clear to me. I fail to see the logic in what you intend to do. The object of disdain is the University as an educational institution, a voice and arm of the Establishment. As such it also represents in large part society as a whole. By altering it you hope it will stimulate change that will reverberate through the entire structure. Then, what is the rationale for reducing this to an individual level? How can you justify a personal situation, a head-on collision with one teacher, as the object of contempt and vindictiveness that is aimed at the larger component? Making one suffer for the sins of the many is contrary to everything we should stand for."

Ted could no longer restrain himself. Not only was he being contradicted and questioned from a source that he never thought would oppose him, but he had to make sure that he did not lose his influence over Chester. In a tone a bit more harsh than he secretly wished, he commenced the destruction of her ideas and comments by ignoring them. "Revolution is not only a war, it is a science. I have studied it that way, and now I will put the centuries of its development to use. The University is the dutiful servant to the power complex, to perpetuate its existence. Education's purposes are merely to train us to receive instructions, follow them, and then keep the records of such obeyed accomplishments. Education should be relevant, and a university should be the place where each generation not only learns to live in harmony with the environment and to contribute to the growth and expansion of society and ideas, but also to develop the conscience of the nation and to supply the impetus and talent to bring about required change. Away from the marketplace morality, the universities are the best place for such clear thinking and for the execution of social action and justice. It is now up to us to bring into fruition the true potential of that role."

Estelle slumped back in her seat drained and exhausted. It was apparent that she had not been effective and that her intentions were being misconstrued. Any comment she could then make would be useless. She had aired her feelings and made a point. Strangely, it was not the result she had intended. She had exerted her independence, a sharp division from Ted's hold on her, and the silence that then hung over them for the remainder of the trip fixed new postures for the three of them. Her crucial year had begun in a flurry of action, too soon to have been planned well and for the necessary follow through that might have really accomplished her tact. She may have even embarked on a course of action leading to no positive result at all. Yet, she had taken the first plunge, finished a first step. Yes, she was doing more than just going back to school. She was going to find out who she was.

SIX

Just recalling that episode left Estelle's youthful spirit depleted. Tomorrow was registration, and although she had meant to contact Dr. Mington upon her return, somehow she knew that she could not face him cognizant of all that was plotted against him. Especially knowing that she was apparently helpless in doing anything about it. Yet, she felt an almost maternal instinct to protect him from harm. She would have to be near him to do that, and merely being in the seminar would not be enough. To be positioned in his office would be a distinct advantage, but a troubling thought prevented her from doing anything about it. She might wind up doing more harm than good. Or was it just that she was afraid to oppose the unanimous force of student opinion and will? No ally had come to her side during the meetings that had taken place over the past few days. The students were much more organized than she had imagined, and she was even more insecure than she cared to be. She was wilting under the force of their combined disapproval. They tolerated her presence at the meetings because of her association with Ted, their revered leader. They listened to her outbursts, but they were deaf to her reasoning. Ted probably permitted her presence and expressions of dissent because they were unpersuasive. He was able to turn her protestations around to add greater emphasis to his urgings and because it lent the appearance of openness at the meetings. He boasted how he welcomed ideas and comments of others, even in contradiction with his plans.

The students were blindly convinced that Ted was right. The inevitable was plotted, and no substantial opposition emerged to channel action in a different direction. The night before she had risen to her feet to try once more to assert her position. It was as if they did not absorb any of the sense she thought she outlined. Even her motives went unappreciated. She was committed to an unpopular cause, and she had the rather unsettling feeling that she was going to suffer more than Dr. Mington. Her supposedly promising future appeared quite cloudy, and from deep within she had a gnawing regret for having spoken up.

Such thoughts were interrupted by a knock on the door. "Yes."

"Telephone," a youthful voice replied.

When she reached the one floor telephone at the end of the hall, the voice that answered her greeting was one she was not prepared for. "Estelle, this is Dr. Mington. I've... I've just been attempting to complete my office work in preparation for registration tomorrow, and since I hadn't heard from you, I was wondering if you had changed your mind about helping me this year?"

His voice had sounded strained. She detected a certain weariness in the tones that made her choke on all of the thoughts and events that would soon touch him so closely and of which he was so innocently unaware. "I apologize, Dr. Mington. There have just been so many things that I have been involved with since I returned. I have been meaning to come over, but there has always been some other pressing matter to take care of."

"Well, then, I gather you still want the non-paying but much appreciated task of being my right hand?"

Decision was thrust upon her. Some mysterious force spurned her on. "Yes."

"That's wonderful. I would hate to break in someone new. I would have to pretend for awhile that I am neat and organized."

"I am happy to spare you of at least that." An instant of silence followed, and she thought and hoped that he might pick up on the provocative statement and question her about it.

He either did not understand that some dire message was hidden in her words, or he chose not to pick up on the lead presented. He cleared his throat, and asked nearly in a whisper, "Now that such formality is over, how was your summer?"

"Oh, fine, I suppose. There were too many things to think about for it to be entirely restful. It seems that the more possibilities that enter into any equation, the slower I am to react and decide."

Again, silence greeted her words. Only the sense that he was still on the line convinced her that he had not hung up. "Dr. Mington, if you would like, I could come over now and give you some help. There must still be much to do for registration tomorrow."

"That would be very nice. I plan to be here for awhile. Perhaps, we can have a moment or two to chat as well."

"I will be there in about twenty minutes."

"Fine. I'll look forward to it."

She heard the click of the receiver, and then hung up stunned by her own actions. Why did she do that? Didn't she want to avoid seeing him until class? It bothered her that she wound up doing something that she had definitely planned not to do. Now, would she have enough sense to handle this meeting with enough reserve so as to warn him about what lay ahead without actually telling him? If she could accomplish that feat, there would be no betrayal of the somewhat warped sense of loyalty she owed to those who had taken her into their confidence.

For Dr. Mington, the reward for the great courage that was required for him to have made the call was immeasurable. Just listening to her voice was joy in itself. The knowledge that she would soon be here led him to ecstatic excitement. He had to stay in control, but for these few moments he wanted to luxuriate in the warmth that quickened his heart beat and emotional thrill that tingled across his body. For this moment in time, here and now, he was young again. He reveled in the magical sensation that invaded his inner and outer being. Its aura dwarfed every other matter in his surroundings both near and far. He would gladly trade everything and everyone in his world for the love of this young woman. He had come to this point on the treadmill to oblivion. There was no turning back, no changing direction. His very sanity hung in the balance.

There was plenty of daylight bathing the campus in its glow. He intently stared for her sight between the partially closed slats of the blind. When her form did appear into view, he felt dizzy. He was completely at the mercy of this personal situation, and totally unsure of himself. Her walk was graceful, and she looked so appealing in the white blouse and plaid skirt. She could not see him, and he took full advantage of being able to stare at her apishly.

When Estelle knocked at the office door, she held her breath. Plots of imaginary conversation ran through her mind if weakness demanded alternatives. She proceeded with caution. To open this door meant closing the last door of retreat behind her. For all of the haste in her wanting to grow up, she felt very inadequate. This was not a child's game. Both physical and mental harms were likely outcomes. Still unsure where she fit in the scheme of things. Was she the potential source for relief or greater damage? She, alone, might be instrumental in the final resolve. A hybrid character in a harsh environment. And, who would spare her? Where would her comfort come from? Where would she be when the final pieces fell into place?

For a tense moment, there was silent acknowledgement of their respective roles. A form of anticipation for an emotional plunge that each, unknown to the other, wished to make but was not totally prepared to do. A pretension of the highest order.

"Estelle, you are looking well." His voice was far steadier than his internal workings would have vented.

She catapulted into what promised to be the most poignant chapter of her life's story so far. "Thank you, I suppose I am well... under the circumstances."

"Sit down. Let's talk for awhile before I ask you to tend to some papers."

She sat down in the chair across from him, and his eyes glanced across the smooth, enticing skin as the skirt rose and she crossed her legs. To avoid looking directly into his eyes, she pretended to look intently at the disarray around the room. "There looks like a lot to do here."

"There is, but most of it can wait. I am sorry to have called you at the dorm, but frankly I was concerned about you. In spite of the numerous outside pressures which we must all deal with, I thought that we had developed a good relationship, a solid rapport."

She looked steadily into the tired eyes. "Yes, we did... I mean, we have. You know I enjoyed assisting you last year. I guess the mood of the times has changed. Change is contagious. As much as I may want to retain the comforts of the past, somehow most of the past does not seem to fit the current picture."

His look was earnest, and his voice sounded sincere. "Why not?"

Her gaze shifted to the window. "I could wax prophetic, like I am no longer master of my own destiny. But, it is far simpler than that. I am just a student, first and foremost a member of the younger generation, the second class citizens. I cannot afford the luxury of trying life out on my own. My life wavelength has been sort of predetermined, at least at this stage of my existence. Their problems collectively become mine individually. The environment is not conducive to any devious schematics or for hearing about ideas or plans that run against that grain. Your world is unsympathetic to this plight. It seems as if no one wants to listen or to make the slightest effort towards understanding the problem. A struggle for ideas on multilevels, with expectations and variations so garbled and intertwined that remedies are lost in the confusion. You, as well as the other elders of our society fail to see the gravity of this situation. There is a war breeding out there. We are in the midst of a great battle of nerves, of clashing principles. You all take it so lightly, as if endurance is the prerequisite for importance. The wait and see technique. If it doesn't go away by itself, perhaps it requires some attention. There is a great deal at stake here. Why doesn't anybody realize it? When it is too late, will you then take it seriously?"

He had not really been prepared for this kind of general onslaught. "I can see that there has been a drastic change in your outlook since we talked last semester. Where is all of the enthusiasm that you had for living? Where is the spirit that you displayed? You were then your own person. You even had me believe that better days lay ahead."

A tear formed in her eye. He was so right. She had changed, not over the period of a few months, but during the past few days. Besides the larger conflict, her own personal war was in full rage. "I guess I have changed. Probably, not for the better. Idealism squandered in the face of practicalities. To reach the future, I have to survive through the present. I see this in no other way than to follow a course that is not my first choice."

A chasm existed between them, and she was acutely aware of it. In spite of the closeness that she had always felt with her family, she had felt that same gap growing with her parents. She did not have to look at Dr. Mington's graying hair or the lines in his face to know it. Differences in age produce more than chronological separations. Too many subtle variations in interpretations of sensory perceptions. Like experiences holding dissimilar meanings and lessons. The need to engage in constant verbal explanations rather than in the unspoken knowing by peers. Sensations and expression without actual communication.   The understanding without having to know. The knowledge without having to be told. Perhaps, older people have the same experiences and feelings, but the frame of reference and meanings are painfully different. The same emotional trains, even possibly with the same destinations, but running on different timetables.

She continued, the pain forming itself into words. "The point of it all. I am a student. You are a teacher. Our roles are different. You do not expect from us what we want from ourselves. In fact, you conspire to prevent us from wanting anything but what you preordain so that we will not disrupt the society that you have inherited. You claim that it is for us, but in reality it is there to ward us off. The pre-built bridges are purposefully narrow, allowing us only to pass on selectively and only a few at a time. The fear of the horde! Perhaps, the fear to face the challenge that you would not or could not face yourselves."

Funny, how she could espouse the cause that she was not totally convinced was right. Stranger still, that the rebellious enchantment came so easily to her lips. Ted would certainly be shocked to hear her echo his sentiments at this point. If this was not her heart or mind speaking, who was the real Estelle? Where had she been? Where was she going? The chill of this inner turmoil made her shudder, the vibrations weakening the very foundation of her being. A terror that she must keep to herself. If it were known that she was so shaken, it would make her an easy prey for disaster.

He gazed at her intently. He looked at this young and wholesome creature before him, and his lips grew dry at the sight of the creamy skin of her bare arms. He longed to hold that slim frame against him, to feel her breasts against his chest. To feel the warmth of her youthful body against his own dilapidated hulk. It was sheer desire, borne from sexual and emotional frustration. A desire to capture what he secretly knew could never be his. This apparently confused child was an object that he wished to possess to help quell his own personal disruptions. To calm his own angry seas. To obliterate his own critical shortcomings. She personified an elixir for his despair. A dream-inspired escape from responsibility and drudgery. It did not matter at all to him about the why or wherefore of generational differences or about the prospects of releasing the young from intellectual bondage. The broader scope of theory was totally irrelevant, but he knew that he had to attempt to release this young woman from the constricting concepts strangling her openness to stand any chance at making a conquest.

Drawing every ounce of mental control from the educator that he used to be, the emotional maturity of the parent that he never was, and the friend that he always was deprived of, he blundered forward in an attempt to turn alienation into reliance. "Estelle, that is some bitter talk. Wars are made by people for selfish and greedy reasons. The ideological war you describe is within some, but not all of us. What about people like you and me? I do not consider myself a combatant, a belligerent in these kinds of hostilities. You, too, recognize that this is not supportive of a growing life. It merely retards it in the guise of progress. Conflict is not the natural relationship between us. It is one that is made, nurtured by demented minds and twisted souls."

She listened dutifully to his words, and her intellect told her that they made sense. She desperately wanted to believe in them. Yet, her belief in right and wrong seemed secondary to her present position. Self-preservation was compelling her to do what she had to do. She was on the fence, and to effectuate her role she had to convince each side that she favored the other. This seemed to be the only way that she might emerge intact. This personal predicament was even more telling now because she felt adherence to the youthful perspective but closer spiritually to this individual man. She did not want to lose his respect and counsel. But, that might have to wait for another time and place.

Her voice was barely audible. "Perhaps, you are right, but even theories can clash. Semantics detract from what we say and what we think we mean. If you were in my place, I suggest you would feel the same as I do."

"I don't believe you really mean that. Nor can I accept it for a moment. Words are merely tools, means by which we disguise or rationalize what we feel. You are a student. I am a teacher. You are a woman. I am a man. Two major differences on the surface. But, are our emotions really that far apart? Do the same situations and impulses leave us both with dissimilar thoughts and consequences? Because of cultural and social divisions, does that mean we are unable to reach a common ground of conscience? Can we not be sympathetic to the other's intent and desire? Does it mean because we bear different labels we cannot be one in the same, by accident or design? Can you do anything or be anyone by merely discarding that label, shedding the false shackles of expectancy and conformity? For every majority, there are general and specific exceptions. Who can know what element in life will turn out to be the most influential and useful one? Let us take an example. Suppose that you and I fell in love and we decided to hell with everything and everybody. Individually, our worlds would probably crumble. I would most likely lose my job. My wife would divorce me. Your family and friends would disdain you. Yet, in spite of all the outward dire effects, would you and I necessarily be worse off? Might not that be the best for us for the moment and for the future? Might it not be better for them all in the long run? Who knows for certain? So, we now have a new struggle. Not between student and teacher, or between a man and a woman, or the old against the young, but rather you and I as one against the rest of the world. Us against them. Isn't that what really counts? For you personally, your action and reaction rather than the general condemnation? To live beyond the social expectancies may be the one way that you can be true to yourself. To do otherwise, is really just to exchange one kind of identifiable, preclassified group for another of the same characteristics. You should not join any group, radical or otherwise, until you yourself are convinced that your goals will not become secondary."

She was not at all sure of the meaning of his words, or where he was taking this discussion. Something lingered in the air, an unspoken tenor that appeared to be beyond a teacher's dangling thought process to be completed by the student's own reasoning so as to solidify the learning process. It confused her. What exactly was he trying to tell her? What was he leading her to say in return? Unfortunately, a further mental strain was not an action she was capable of at the moment.

Her silence frightened him. He did not want to lose her under the weight of coming on too strong. He had hopefully planted a seed, and he would have to be patient to enjoy the flowering.

Patience is a tree with bitter roots that bears sweet fruit [China].

She did not know what to say, and in the awkwardness of the moment rather than say anything she stood up as if the conversation was never held and began to straighten up the office. Silently, he joined in.

They did not speak further at any length, and by the time that she left, Estelle felt somewhat relieved. Her busy fingers had brought on a physical weariness that temporarily supplanted her active mind. As she headed for the dining room for supper, she felt her resolve stronger than ever. Discovering that Dr. Mington would not be leading the seminar might prove to be a quick answer to the immediate danger, although she would not undervalue Ted's cunning ability to adjust to change. She did feel better, knowing that there might be some hope that she need not be an active participant in the ensuing drama.

For him, as he watched her walk away, he felt numb. His despair filled him with a crying loneliness, and he did not have to be the greatest intellect to know that he was slowly losing his grip on matters. Vestiges of a meaningful and sane life were fleeting away, and he was hapless. His road was leading to oblivion. Nothing could or would change that.

SEVEN

The first day of classes was particularly uneventful. For Ted Amherst and his following it was a time of watchful waiting. The seminar was not scheduled until the next day. Once they had accepted the fact that Dr. Mington would not be in charge of that meeting, they decided that for their purposes a new professor might even prove better. Especially, this Justin Post, who enjoyed a national reputation, and who might be more newsworthy. Their task would be simple. All that they had to do was to attend the seminar and mold their human catalyst to their will.

The one added benefit that Ted thought would emerge did not materialize. Once Dr. Mington was removed from the picture, he thought that Estelle's objections and obstinacy would dissipate. He thought that she was just trying to protect the good doctor as an individual she knew and respected. He had diagnosed the situation as one in which she felt indebted to him for the guidance he had given her. However, he was wrong about that. Estelle's opposition had grown even more adamant over the days since registration. He allowed her to sit in on the planning sessions, hoping that she would come to her senses or that she would be persuaded of the folly of her ways. Yet, she did not listen in silence. He began to resent her frequent outspoken interjections of contrariness. An underlying antagonism towards him became evident, and he was really perplexed in deciding what should be done with her. After all, she was his girl, and she had no right to stand up against him. She had never done so before this recent period, and he had felt confident that he had mastered her mind as well as her body.

Now that she refused to have anything to do with him physically, and would not even agree to see him alone, he had to contend with her unemotionally, if he could. He would simply put her out of his personal life and deal with her in the setting of her own choosing, as an adversary. She might even be useful to him if manipulated properly. He could not discount her entirely, but as long as she did not actually persuade any of the others to abandon his coat tails and join her in opposition, he would tolerate her presence and outrage. It might add some fuel to the fire. Her isolated resistance actually gave added conviction to his contentions. Her presence in the seminar would also be a valuable ploy. He would not hesitate to use or sacrifice her for the cause he espoused, even though deep down he longed for a gentle, peaceful moment with the warmth of her body as the sensory point for such solitude.

Estelle literally dragged herself through three classes that first day, not daring to contribute anything to them and carefully avoiding mixing with those she knew to be associated with Ted. Her perplexity had grown to the point where she felt more vulnerable than ever. She had not slept or eaten well. In the silent confinement of her room where she did not have to portray an image of strength, her staunch resolve quivered and her nerves were frayed. She was definitely beginning to break apart, and the strain was building moment by moment.

Tomorrow was the marked seminar, and she was at a total loss as to how she might cope with it. She had clearly defined her position to the others, and this was tolerated although she no longer fully understood why. Apparently, nobody assumed she would stand in his or her way outside of the private meetings. She knew that she could not stand up against any onslaught on her own. Yet, she sensed a subtle but urgent reaching out for help by this Justin Post, and she was determined to help him if she could. What plan she might devise to offset the possible destruction of a man's integrity, a university's downfall, and still manage to preserve her own crumbling world, appeared monumental in scope.

Her torment increased through the day and into the early evening. She could not keep her mind on the first study assignments. By ten o'clock, the closeness of her four walls pressed down on her. She left for a walk, heading for a small coffee shop a few blocks away that was open all night.

Another problem was bothering her. Dr. Mington had changed. She was frightened by his bold attitude. Inwardly, it upset her while also thrilling her in the sense that she had never been the object of attraction by an older man. There was a degree of provocativeness in such a situation. But, she did not know how to handle it, and she could not explain the drastic alteration in his mannerism. A certain repulsion overtook any arousal she might have felt. She did not want to help him in the office again. She did not want to have anything to do with him. How to accomplish that feat also presented major obstacles to any possible free flowing course of her life.

Estelle, of course, did not know the true depth of Dr. Mington's agony. He was as close to decay as any man could get and still go on. On that first day, he carefully avoided any contact with student or faculty member alike. As he leaned back in the chair in his quiet office, his bosom filled with self-pity. From a stance in his life where he had nothing, everything turned repeatedly sour.

After the reunion with Estelle, he had felt better. For a brief time he had a belief that he might still be in control of his life. Little did he count on what would confront him at home. That night, Henrietta completely and coldly rejected his attempted overtures of concern. She had been drinking, and would listen to no appeals. A violent argument ensued, one in which she let out all of the pent-up disgust she felt towards him as a husband and father. Nothing he could say would placate her. Accusations and insults were cast at him. There was no choice but to leave the house.

The next day, he tried to telephone her, but before she slammed down the receiver she yelled at him to not bother coming back. He was no longer welcome there. It was the physical termination of his home. It was no less than he deserved, but it came in the face of what might have been his last capable attempt to do something right. It left him hanging with nothing at all. Any remaining chance to recapture some dignity was smothered.

By the next time that Estelle had come to the office to help, he was totally victimized by emotional instability. He desired her with such a great force that it obsessed him with its urgency. His longing for her was the last gasp of a dying man. He was desperate. Only the crowd in the building prevented him from grabbing her right then and there. How to get her to the apartment near the campus that he had been forced to move to became the focal point of his pursuit. Let his body conquer her, and he would prove to Henrietta and to the world that he was just as much a man as the rest of them. He had regressed to animalistic thoughts and behavior. His hold on living was quickly slipping away from him. Selfishness drove him to lust for a moment of glory. That he might also destroy this young woman no longer mattered. After all, it was her fault that he had come to this. It would, inescapably, prove that his ruin was not entirely of his own doing.

It was also a very restless evening for Justin Post. Too many disjointed thoughts had been going through his mind in rapid succession to enable him to calmly slip into extended periods of work. Mainly, it was the anticipation of tomorrow's seminar that disquieted him. His initiation into a world he had only known at the other end. An unknown promise for him to keep. A situation and participants were looming as unpredictable. To be no longer on the sidelines, but thrust on to the field of action was not very reassuring. A dreamer confronting the reality before the dream.

He had been quite disturbed since registration. The picketing by the students coupled with an apparent hostile attitude toward the school authority, filled the air with tension. There appeared to be a concerted action to avoid and depersonalize all contacts between the registering students and the school officials. Prescribed routine shifted into chaos.

One student that he did talk to appeared to have a different attitude. Estelle Winslow, who was helping at the Department table, through some cryptic conversation seemed more willing to be cooperative and communicative. He even had the distinct impression that there was some concern on her part for what was going on around them. He had a strange feeling that in some way she was trying to tell him something. Perhaps, to warn him of pitfalls and dangers that threatened the course of events. Not that he needed that extra warning. He sensed it on his own. It might have been just that apprehension that gave him that impression of her behavior. However, there was an unusual blend in her mannerism of friendliness and a kind of desperation, and it baffled him.

He tried to direct his mind to more pleasant thoughts. The memory of last evening when he had dinner at Kate's apartment. The easy smile that came to her full lips, blending graciously with her facial expressions and the smooth skin of her cheeks. Kate was a genuine person, an individual full of life. Multitalented and multifaceted, leaving him totally enchanted by her diversity of means and her personal drive. Her paintings adorned the walls. Each meal she had prepared was a culinary masterpiece. Knowing that he had not yet pierced the deep inner characteristics, he was still quite taken by all of the outward strengths displayed when necessary. Above all, he was very grateful for her presence in his life at this guarded moment. Just when he needed a person with emotional stability and a flare for life, she seemed to provide those attributes and more.

Unfortunately, that pleasant feeling faded as his mind reached further back in time to a similar personal relationship, one that did not fare so well. It was through Rosalind that he had come to believe in love at first sight, and if they had been alone in the world that might never have changed. Its development would have been unburdened, providing enough of an impetus to carry them to whatever heights beckoned. Total commitment would not have been subjected to outside pressures. The magical enchantment might have been eternal.

Justin had drowned in his own personal ineptitude, been swallowed up by his own warped perceptions of what others had expected of him. While he should only have cared about what he could expect from himself, and to satisfy the pure and honest demands of this loving relationship, he got caught in an undercurrent which carried him away from reality, away from the happiness he could have dwelled in. He could not muster the courage or energy to right that situation before it drifted beyond repair. He lost her, lost the chance, and wound up fighting the very world he thought he was conforming to. Finding only frustration in failing on all fronts. That personal tragedy was all of his own doing, and the guilt he felt about it was debilitating. He felt badly for himself, worse for her. Her suffering and hurt were at his hands. His thoughtlessness and lack of consideration compounded the deed. His finest moment vanquished by his own action. What a testament to a romantic's folly! It could never be made up to her, even if he ever found her. He was even unsure at this moment whether he could offset its effect on himself. This obstacle to his own release from the emotional bondage of his being. He was not a confident captain of his life's ship. The potential of a mental sanctuary seemed too remote. His direction and dedication to it would be haphazard at best. No real promise of a safe harbor, merely the perpetual rise and fall in the swells of circumstance.

No wonder his whole entity was replete with agitation and anxiety. The precarious edge he had situated himself on did not afford him the possibility of calmness. It would take much more than he seemed ready to put forward to emerge from this test of his worth as a better person. He might very well have to achieve that before he could rescue society so ravaged by fears and doubts. His book would prove ineffective if he could not exude the power of a path clearer. Perhaps, when all was said and done, he was the greatest symptom of the disease.

Even at the coffee shop, Estelle could not escape the echo chamber in her head. It was almost as if she could see a face in the coffee in the cup, her own face but nearly unrecognizable. The representation of her predicament was strong and shook her insides. She knew who she was and that she was here, but in a relatively brief period of time, she had lost the capacity to believe in herself. The warm vapor from the coffee caressed her lips, and she was surprised that she could feel that, to feel anything at all.

The place was nearly deserted, and she slumped dejectedly into the cushion in the last booth in the rear of the shop. Staring into the obscured depths of the cup, she did not notice the presence of Justin Post by the table until he spoke. "A quarter for your thoughts?"

Estelle glanced up, and the sight of the gentle and warm face brought an instant smile to her lips. Instinctively, a hand went up to check that her hair was neatly in place. "A penny will do," she said, gesturing with her hand for him to sit across from her.

He sat down, placed his elbows comfortably on the table, and peered deeply into her sparkling eyes. "Besides the rate of inflation, you seemed so far away in thought that it looks like even a quarter would be quite a bargain."

"You might find it to be the costliest twenty-five cents you ever spent."

He reached into his pocket, placed a quarter before her, motioned to the waitress for a cup of coffee, and returned to gaze into those clear eyes. "Let me be the judge of that."

This unplanned opportunity propelled her into a further commitment. "It's about the seminar." She hesitated, waiting for some reaction to show itself in his face. Nothing that she could detect.

The waitress brought the coffee. Justin wondered why Estelle had stopped so abruptly, and he had an urge to pick up on the thread and reveal his exasperation on this topic. Prudence dictated that he hear her out first.

She waited until he had taken a sip of the coffee. Whether or not what she was going to say was going to come out the right way, if there was a right way, did not seem as important as the fact that it would be said. "I suppose these are puzzling times for many of us. Such uncertainty with everything we have taken for granted. The students are restless and demanding. They can also be cunning, verging on brutality. An overt display of their power is in the works. A sacrifice, albeit a mental rather than a physical one, is desired. It will not be one of their own. The administration of the college is targeted for such a victim." Again she paused, seeking some reaction in his expression or mannerism. There was no visible break in the intentness of his look.

Although Justin's exterior was placid, his insides had tightened. Actually, he was not being told anything that he had not figured out for himself. Dr. Mington had already informed him that potential ringleaders had collectively enrolled in the seminar, and that it could not be for any constructive purpose. Yet, hearing this unmistakable confirmation of his apprehension was not without an internal reaction, an intestinal anxiety. "And that object is me," he said, as if finishing her remarks on cue.

"Yes. I am afraid it is. At first, they had picked out Dr. Mington. Then, they convinced themselves that a new professor would be better. There is really nothing personal directed towards you, as foolish as that sounds. It is just your unfortunate place in the scheme of things. A cold, methodical, matter-of-fact choice. For you, just being in the wrong place at the wrong time."

"Estelle," mustering every ounce of concentration to attempt to convey an image of unperturbness, "I know that it has not been easy for you to tell me this. I really appreciate it. It was something I have sort of figured out for myself, and there is still the option of canceling the seminar. I guess that would again remove an opportunity for them, besides letting me off the hook. But, I am not sure that would solve anything. Another plan will take its place, one that might be more destructive. I certainly don't want to give you the impression that I am a hero dressed up in professor's clothing, or anything crazy like that. If the truth were known, I am very much afraid of it all, and it is nothing I want and everything I would like to avoid. I have done a number of foolish things in my life, and this will probably rank first at the head of that long list. But, at the moment, simply because I am so new and relatively detached in the sense that any loyalties for the university are not yet entrenched, I will go ahead with the seminar. Tomorrow, before it begins, I may wish otherwise. Right now, at personal risk, I think I might have more to lose by backing out than by plodding ahead. I don't know if you understand when I say this is a situation that I cannot turn my back on. I assume you will not go along with their plan since you have divulged all this to me. So, let me be very honest with you. I don't know what will happen tomorrow. I am at a loss on how to handle it. I am just going to do what I had originally thought of doing. I am going to present a mental challenge to them, and hope they take the bait."

She was surprised at how relaxed she was starting to feel. It was easy to talk to him, and it was a relief to release the pent-up feelings harbored within. "They know how I feel. I am not sure of all the details of what is contemplated, but I know they are going to give you as difficult a time as possible, including discussing only what they want to discuss."

"Sounds just great! Do you have any suggestions as to how I might handle it?"

"I don't really know. The first few minutes might be crucial. If you can set the subject or pace, it might throw them off balance. I'll try to help you as much as I can, if I can. These past few days, I have discovered that I am much weaker than I want or need to be. Whatever I think… whatever I say… I cannot shake the sense that they are really me, in mass form, and that I cannot stand up to them just as I cannot fully oppose myself. That may not make much sense listening to it, but it as close as I can describe it."

He was silent for a moment, and pensive. "Strange, how for both of us this represents a personal challenge, perhaps of monumental proportions."

She nodded her head in agreement. The warmth spread over her body, and she found a will of dedication flowing through her extremities. The situation may not be as overwhelming or helpless as she had thought. Here was someone who believed that this need not be an all or nothing situation. Maybe, the secret was not to succeed but merely to get through it. Beyond tomorrow, if she could afford the luxury of thinking that far ahead, there might be a glimmer of a future for her. Perhaps, it was just waiting there for her, and all that she had to do was to get there. An added emotional dimension gave her comfort. If she could get to that destination, Justin might be there too.

Justin fought against a compelling urge to reach out and touch the delicate hand that rested on the table. She was no ordinary woman, and he wanted to know more about her. "You don't have to talk about this, but I am very curious as to how you came to this point in time and your relation to it."

She looked at his hands on the table. They appeared strong and supportive, and she wished that he would grasp her with them. Possibly, she could derive some badly needed strength from them. "That is a long story."

"I told you I would get a bargain for my twenty-five cents!"

She smiled, and the last vestige of containment flittered away in a sigh. She had found someone to talk to, someone she wanted to talk to, and someone she knew would listen while caring. Now, it would all get told. Her commitment had carried her to a new plateau. And talk she did. At great length, she described all of the events that had taken place since that fateful car ride back to the school, as well as all of her reactions to the happenings and the people. She even told all of the details of what had transpired with Dr. Mington and the impression she had as to what he wanted from her. No verbal reaction was needed during the outpouring. The understanding and concern were written on his face. She felt it most strongly when he reached over and covered her hand with his. An enchanting novelty for her to communicate on such a level. She was relishing it.

When he did speak, the voice solidified the magical aura. "For awhile, I thought I was the only one with a difficult predicament, with burdensome problems. I feel your plight more than I can express in words. Maybe, we can get a little solace and courage from each other."

She did not know exactly how to react to his words. She did know that she liked the warmth of his hand on hers and the slight reassuring pressure of his long fingers. She had an urge to lay her head on his shoulder. She was very tired, but no longer without hope. By an unusual combination of events, this young man had been catapulted into a paramount place in her life. She was not surprised, and even delighted, to feel that presence deep in her heart.

Justin walked her back to the dormitory. They parted at some distance from the building, knowing that prying eyes might not be far off. The bond between them, however, had been fused. They would not be able to coordinate their efforts for the seminar's ordeal. Yet, there was a definite conceptual unity of purpose from which they could reap support.

As he walked back to his apartment, Justin was struck by the similarity between many of Estelle's expressions and mannerisms and those of Rosalind's. Or, was he just imagining this? As he had listened to her speak, it had brought back vivid memories of the many times that they had engaged in close and lengthy conversations. The many times that he had sat back listening to Rosalind's vibrant voice revealing an emotional discourse of a young girl's impressions of life and people.

A new element was present in the course of his life. Estelle had emerged as an additional test for his personal existence. As George Sand said so aptly, *We know whom it is we have lost, we cannot tell whom we may find.* The seminar and his relationship with the people he now knew were one, intertwined as an unforgiving trial for the meaning and progress of his development. The genesis of his new book was dominant in the life bearing down on him. How to approach it all would be difficult. Each deed, each thought, each feeling goes in two ways – to the separate parts as well as to the whole picture, to the whole person.

EIGHT

The classroom was probably no different than most. A rectangular box, rows of seats, a desk in front. The glare of fluorescent lights casting bright but unreal illumination upon the staid setting. As he sat behind the desk waiting for the students to enter, the silence was almost soothing to the internal agitation he was feeling. Seventeen registered students, one teacher.

Justin knew what had to be done. The confrontation would be a great challenge for his young years, his inexperience before and with a group. It would be more than an outward conflict. The students no longer represented solely an opposing force. Rather, they had become an outward extension of his own being – the pulsating, disquieting spirit that all frustrations and disappointments would gravitate to. The battle was not really between teacher and student, as they believed it to be. It was the Justin Post of now against the Justin Post of yesterday. What was going to emerge from this conflict was not going to be either impulse or reason, but an enigma of the Justin Post of tomorrow. He did not fear the demise of his former being. He was apprehensive about the new form that would take hold.

As if each breath that he took had a significance of its own, the minutes passed slowly, agonizingly. Increased movement was evident in the hallway. Students changing classes. Some off to an exciting or stimulating introduction to academic knowledge; some off to the start of another dull experience to wade through, to tolerate. Moments to be endured rather than spent growing. Stimulation a lost commodity. Curiosity a bare whisper in the wind that brushes the skin, leaving the trace of a tingle but nothing to hold on to. The students did have a basic justification for their attitude and desire for change. Cause plus concern should prompt action. Overlooked, perhaps, the choice of remedies.

The door opened, and they entered as if they were one. Color and form blending into a unified solid display of presence. Thirteen young men and four young women. Each, except for one, appraising him as they filled all of the seats in the rear of the room thereby leaving four vacant rows as a buffer zone. An initial move to unnerve him, to swing the opening advantage to their favor.

Motionless, silent, wide-eyed. Their gaze penetrating to his volcanic inner workings while they maintained a stone-like exterior. He peered back, roaming from face to face. Ordinary faces. Young people banded together in collectiveness for what they believed to be a higher cause. Who could doubt their sincerity? Little would they know that he was secretly on their side. As Helen Swick Perry said in her 1970 book, The Human Be-In: *In American society, we seem to have a built-in crisis in the adolescent years for everyone; in an atomic age, this crisis has escalated, and the words "kill" and "overkill" threaten all of springtime.*

He glanced quickly at Estelle's face. The eyes sparkled with held-back tears, and the feeling for his plight filled her cheeks.

As the staring game proceeded, he broke away to the papers before him on the desk. He read in the steadiest voice that he could muster.

Oh, man in your individuality! Can it be that you have rotted in this baseness for sixty centuries? You call yourself pure and sacred, but you are only the whore, the sucker, the goat of your servants, your monks, and your mercenary soldiers. You know this and you endure it! To be GOVERNED is to be kept under surveillance, inspected, spied upon, bossed, law-ridden, regulated, penned in, indoctrinated, preached at, registered, evaluated, appraised, censured, ordered about, by creatures who have neither the right, nor the knowledge, nor the virtue to do so. To be GOVERNED is to be at each operation, at each transaction, at each movement, marked down, recorded, inventoried, priced, stamped, measured, numbered, assessed, licensed, authorized, sanctioned, endorsed, reprimanded, obstructed, reformed, rebuked, chastised. It is, under the pretense of public benefit and in the name of the general interest, to be requisitioned, drilled, fleeced, exploited, monopolized, extorted, squeezed, hoaxed, robbed; then at the slightest resistance, the first word of complaint, to be squelched, corrected, vilified, bullied, hounded, tormented, bludgeoned, disarmed, strangled, imprisoned, shot down, judged, condemned, deported, sacrificed, sold, betrayed, and to top it off, ridiculed, made a fool of, outraged, dishonored. That's government, that's its justice, that's its morality!

"Right on!" A solitary voice responded. Then a hushed silence.

"A form of literary masterpiece. Does anyone know who the author is?" Nothing. But, he held their eyes.

"Pierre-Joseph Proudhon in 1851. He was one of the first so-called modern anarchists. Yes, an anarchist! Not a dirty word. It is what you all are. What I probably am as well. Do you know what anarchy really is? What it means? Do you care to know? Does it shock you to know that more than a hundred years ago there were people who think the way that you do now?"

There was no response to the questions fired off in rapid succession. Bodies rustled in their seats and heads turned towards one young man in the back row.

Justin sensed that he had gained an initial upper hand. Now it was his to hold and to use cautiously.

The youth rose slowly to his feet, dramatically using the expectation that filled the air as a general might use the anticipation before a major battle. In the moment before he spoke, Justin observed the young man's features. A strong nose, attentive but squinting eyes, and a mouth just a bit too small for the long face. The lips thin, pinched-looking. Tall, slim, crowned with thick curly black hair.

"This is a seminar," the young man began in a voice slightly louder than necessary for the small room. "We have sat through lectures, year-upon-year, silent and intent on absorbing the rules and procedures devised by others, decided by others to be in our best interest. No longer! No more! We are escaping the imprisonment of ideas, and here we will decide what is to be expressed, and exactly what is to be done. This is our forum. You be the student. We will do the teaching. Listen to us, and you will learn as you never have before. Call it anarchism, socialism, humanitarianism, or what-ever you like. What significance is there in a label anyway? Listen to the truth, stripped of the artificial adornments of the eggheads. Refute it if you can. If you dare!"

"Bravo!" The voices chimed in unison. Their spokesman had shown his stuff, made his mark. The eyes now riveted on Justin Post, the audacious professor. Would he have the nerve to respond? What could he say to negate the stated agenda?

"No!" His voice ringing with adamancy. "That's not an arrangement I will accept. Let's go one step further…if you dare…and not only attempt to reach the real meaning of a seminar but also carry into action the logical extension of your own idea. Let's have no teacher, no students. Let's all be equal. No role playing, and really see if one or all of us can learn that way. Outside any prescribed pattern or practice." There he paused, sensing that he had scored again.

"Accepted," the youth shouted out jumping to his feet. Ted Amherst real-ized, reluctantly, that he had a greater match here than he wished for, far more than he had expected. Now, to infuse a little drama into the situation. "We'll even be gracious enough to let you have the floor first, with the pro-viso that you don't get carried away with artificial brilliance."

Justin sat down on the edge of the desk. Quickly, he scanned Estelle's face, not long enough to be sure that it was a trace of a smile that appeared on her lips. "I agree with you," he began slowly, employing every tactic he had ever known about debating and advocacy to hold the attention of the audience. "A title or label for ideas is unimportant compared to the princi-ples involved. Yet, a title is interesting in the sense that in a historical per-spective there may have been prior times when others wanted to react, or did in fact react, the way you or I may want to. Is there really anything new under the sun? Whether the reasons are different or not, how similar are the ideas, the aspirations? Rebelliousness, love of freedom, individualism, love of one's neighbors, sensitiveness, sense of justice, sense of logic, a desire for knowledge. Any or all of these. These are concepts that a label can be affixed to so that our somewhat restricting language can conveniently describe them so that a full explanation does not have to be offered each time an idea reemerges. I used the word anarchism as being the term, a shorthand convenience, for a political theory at some earlier time that closely fits to what I think you all feel. If the proverbial shoe fits, why not wear it? Max Stirner, a self-proclaimed anarchist who ardently believed in absolute freedom of the individual devised what he called an *association of egoists* in which individuals can freely enter to pursue their particular interests, and then leave whenever they like. In effect, isn't that what we are proposing here? An association of egoists."

Ted rose to his feet again. With deliberate motion, he walked to the desk and then to the window. He clasped his hands behind him, and still looking out the window as if peering into eternity and addressing the world at large, he spoke knowing full well that no one would interrupt him. The chosen leader would be expected to deflate the rising balloon, and swing the current of approval in his direction. His own oratory would not be daunted by this fast-talking, glib pseudo-intellectual. "I am an IBM card. I am a DO NOT FOLD, BEND OR SPINDULATE piece of paper. Prerecorded. Precoded. Ejected, as a reject from the machine into a world which itself is a reject. A mad, cruel, unreasoning universe. All around us are the imponderables and inconsistencies of our elders. A hot war. A cold war. Stepped on by pretension; spit on by the threat of nuclear holocaust; pissed on by a defouled environment; and shit on by an abused technology. Forced to live in a messed-up world which we had no part in creating, and if they would have it their way, we would be useless to change it. Letting us think that we can do something while at the same time daunting and diminishing any power to do it. Guy Strait sums it up well in <u>What is a Hippie?</u>, *The straight world is a jungle of taboos, fears, and personality games. . . . The oldest fallacy in the world is that anything that makes you angry must be bad.* Hope. The greatest hoax of them all. Our elders, the establishment, to employ your labeling technique, a morass of swine, filth, deceit, cheating, corruption, lies, and propaganda. A complete disruption is the only way to change a decadent society. Beneath my punched-out holes, a vestige of flesh and blood exists. A faint heart beats. Whatever is left of me, I dedicate it to the new holy trinity – LIFE, LOVE, and LEARNING."

"Hooray! Hooray!" The throng cheered. Anyone passing in the hall would probably think that a pep rally was being held inside, not a purported classical seminar.

Sensing that the full impact was accomplished, Ted turned to the desk, to the upstart teacher. He saw no panic, no defeat in the young professor's face. Knowing that he could not outstare those steady eyes, he made his way back to his seat, getting encouraging pats along the way.

Justin Post was keen enough to know that this was a turning point. It would have been easy to blast away at that flowery presentation, to riddle it or ridicule it, separating as a conclusion the differences between form and substance. But, to do just that might easily lead to the impression of a personal attack on the young man himself. It was paramount that this discussion, which had gotten off to an intellectual beginning, remain that way. In fact, he would take the long road to make sure that it did not degenerate into a mud-slinging attack. He would wait a few minutes before speaking to allow the young student to bask in his aura a bit longer. A shrewd form of subtle ingratiation.

"In anarchist theory," he began, emphasizing each word in turn while looking into the transfixed eyes before him, "revolution means the moment when the structure of authority is loosened so that free functioning can occur. In this forum, we cannot tackle all of the problems confronting society, but I propose we try an experiment. Let's try to create in these weekly meetings a revolution of that sort in our immediate world. Realistically, if it doesn't work in here, it won't work out there."

Ted was on his feet with a quick retort. "You are very fond of labels and proposals, aren't you? O.K. We'll call it a revolution. And, if that is what it is, it will not work in here. Besides what your presence symbolizes, even if you say you will abandon it for the here and now, the vent of our anger is against what lies out there. The grand scheme. It is a revolution aimed not against our fellow human beings but against a system, one that is impersonal, inhuman, illogical, incompetent, and inconsistent."

The pace was picking up. Justin knew that he could not concentrate on both the direction and the tempo of the confrontation at this point. Instantly, he chose to champion the former and sacrifice the latter. His words came out rapidly and forcefully. "That, my friend, is to encourage neglect of doing what is possible under the pretext of waiting for the impossible. You speak of your holy trinity. I speak and profess for us here the four principles long and urgently professed by the anarchists. These concepts are JUSTICE, VIRTUE, TRUTH, and BROTHERHOOD. If we cannot find and foster them here, they for sure can never exist in the abyss beyond this room."

Ted plopped into his seat, and with a wave of his hand dismissed the words flung at him. It was, however, obvious that the others were enjoying the repartee. They had come to witness a trouncing, and had so far found an even match.

Realizing that he might not be able to outtalk this arrogant professor, Ted suddenly grew quiet, displaying an air of disinterest bordering on boredom. Justin pounced on the opportunity. He exclaimed, embracing the entire room with his voice, "Would anyone else like to add a thought?" Thus, here was a new challenge, an invitation to participate. Without that it would be an affront to Ted for any of them to have spoken up. After all, they were a loyal hodge-podge of growing, yearning weeds.

A young man, a wisp of blond hair shielding all of one eye, spoke out in a nasal voice. "Sure, I would like to find these things. But what good is it here? This is an unreal world. The evils are beyond this campus – corporate and political conglomerates, artificial social pressures, brain washing by the media, criminal activities by multinational corporations in other countries, the false grandeur of suburbia. All of the bureaucrats are peddlers of false dreams and hopes. The list is endless."

Justin Post looked at the young man. "Yes. That may be true generally, and it probably is best summed up in something that George Bernard Shaw wrote with a tongue-in-cheek technique. He may very well have been one of you today, or even me. Anyway, I would like to read it to you. Perhaps, it ties together everything we have started to talk about.

"Yes," cries some eccentric individual; "but all this is untrue of me. I want to marry my deceased wife's sister. I am prepared to prove that your authorized system of medicine is nothing but a debased survival of witchcraft. Your schools are machines for forcing spurious learning on children in order that your universities may stamp them as educated men when they have finally lost all power to think for themselves. The tall silk hats and starched linen shirts which you force me to wear, and without which I cannot successfully practice as a physician, clergyman, schoolmaster, lawyer, or merchant, are inconvenient, unsanitary, ugly, pompous, and offensive. Your temples are devoted to a God to whom I do not believe; and even if I did believe in him I should still regard your popular forms of worship as only redeemed from gross superstition by their obvious insincerity. Science teaches me that my proper food is good bread and good fruit; your boasted food supply offers me cows and pigs instead. Your care for my health consists in tapping the common sewer, with its deadly typhoid gases, into my house, besides discharging its contents into the river, which is my natural bath and fountain. Under color of protecting my person and property you forcibly take my money to support an army of soldiers and policemen for the execution of barbarous and detestable laws; for the waging of wars which I abhor; and for the subjection of my person to those legal rights of property which compel me to sell myself for a wage to a class the maintenance of which I hold to be the greatest evil of our time. Your tyranny makes my very individuality a hindrance to me: I am outdone and outbred by the mediocre, the docile, the time-serving. Evolution under such conditions means degeneracy: therefore I demand the abolition of all of the officious compulsions, and proclaim myself an Anarchist."

The silence in the room displayed rapt attention. He continued, tying the loose ends together, "There will always be major problems, differences, disappointments and failures in our society. Yet, changing them is much more important than merely condemning them. I still maintain that if we make the effort, some of the changes can start right here."

Another youth spoke out, the voice somewhat tentative. "I'd rather think of us as a counter-culture than as anarchists. We are different from the anarchists in their hay day. Our movement is youth-oriented, and if my understanding is correct, pure anarchism is inter-generational."

Fortunately, this was an area that Justin was well versed in. "Yes, that is true, but there are not only enough similarities between your views and the anarchists of old, much of the feelings evident in today's occurrences are tinged with traditional anarchist overtones. Examples would include the acceptance of violence, radical criticism of the technological state, the rejection of majoritarianism, the insistence on the moral responsibility of the individual, the asceticism towards property, the desire to simplify life, and the deep sense of frustration at the intractability of the main culture. The anarchist assumption is that the individual is both responsible and free, and the belief is that if one man opposes the system it is possible that others will and the system can be stopped. Hits pretty close to home, doesn't it? Anyway, especially pertinent, as I view it, is the anarchist millennial vision of a day in which a young child finds two words in a book – *oppressor* – and *oppressed* – and the child asks you what those two words mean and you can't point to a goddamn thing in the world to cite as an example. Which really leads to a more important question. In spite of the differences, what is the relevance of anarchism as a living tradition, especially for us? The importance is probably the element of belief that a few on the margin can define the morality for the whole of society. Theodore Roszak, in his 1968 book, The Making of a Counter Culture, describes your culture as being so radically disaffiliated from the mainstream assumption of our society that it scarcely looks to many as a culture at all, but takes on the alarming appearance of a barbaric intrusion. So, to many people counter culture or anarchism, whatever you call it, represents a total absence of order. It is chaos or nihilism. We know otherwise. But, what is the most effective way of sharing this view with others? Can they be persuaded? Would they be convinced of any redeeming features of such a cause? It is not unreasonable that the movement for correction in this arena is in the universities. Here, where knowledge is sought and intellectual priorities established, where theoretically potential and promise can flourish unimpeded, and where one can relate the wisdom of the past and experiment in fitting it to the problems of the present and future, is where the ideas and roles can be built, altered, or destroyed. That is why I still urge that we can do so much here. If you want to change the world we live in, and if it can best be accomplished by piecemeal social engineering, the first step is with yourselves. Then, you can proceed along the pattern of George Sorel's hypothesis if you want to. If you believe in something hard enough, if you create the impression that there is going to be a revolution, if you spread the conviction that society is rotten to the core and is about to collapse, then you have already taken a big step forward to that collapse. A myth, or not, isn't it worth finding out? Belief in the possibility of the impossible can sometimes be as vital as action itself. In a communiqué distributed by the Diggers on Haight Street, haunting words enflame reality. *Enlightenment, described in many tongues and in many ways, teaches, among other truths, that truly to feel the unity of all men that is love requires the giving up of the illusion of game-playing abstractions.*"

Justin paused, and the enthralled silence hung over him as if it were a cape. "Enough to digest for one meeting. If you read more about all of this, we will easily escape the traditional teacher-student display, and you can well lead me as well. I move to adjourn our society of egoists."

The students filed out quietly, pensively. The seminar was over. He had been totally convincing to them and to himself. In a way, he was learning from them, and he hoped that they were starting to think about matters all over again. It had not turned out as he or they had expected. He was not sure whether that was a good result in the long run. He did know that his ghosts of yesterday now seemed very distant. The book was being written in the doing.

NINE

A man half as desperate might well have concocted the same plot. It was so logical, so perfect that it could not fail. When Justin Post had told him all that had transpired in the seminar that day, and that Estelle was his ally, Dr. Mington quickly devised a plausible scheme to get Estelle to his apartment that night. About eight o'clock, he telephoned her at the dormitory and told her that he and Justin were going to have a meeting at nine o'clock to discuss further tactics. He gave her the address and apartment number without telling her that it was his apartment. Even when she told him that she had spoken to Justin on the telephone about an hour before and that he had not mentioned such a meeting, he was persuasive in telling her that it was a decision just made and that Justin was going to the faculty office to get some notes.

Long voyages – great lies [Italy].

While Estelle should have been more suspicious of this arrangement, and even though she would have exercised a much greater degree of caution under another set of circumstances, she was so heartened by recent developments and so elated and enraptured by Justin that even the remotest connection between him and an event or activity immediately clothed it with sanctity. So, she left her room for the meeting without giving more thought to it than the pleasant expectation that she would be in his company. Swept up by emotion, the heart and mind do not function in unison. Lost to her, the expectancies held her at their mercy. The greatest moment of strength often is the most vulnerable for defeat.

Dr. Mington answered her knock. She looked by him into the small room for Justin. He was not there.

"Justin just called to say he had been delayed, and will get here as soon as he can."

She entered the apartment, and he closed and locked the door behind her. Looking around at the faded furniture, particularly at the small bed in the cramped quarters, she wondered who really lived here. She remarked innocently, "Ominous events could result from meeting in a place like this."

"Perhaps they will," was his quick retort.

There being no place else to sit comfortably, she sat upon the bed crossing her legs under her.

"I have some gin here," he said softly, "Would you like a drink?"

Normally, she would have refused. She had never developed a taste for alcohol. She drank now and then to be sociable, and never went out of her way to have a drink. Now, it sounded like a good idea. After all, some celebration for the victory of the day was appropriate.

It was fortuitous that she could not see his hands trembling as he went to the small refrigerator and took out some ice cubes from the tray. Now that he had her here, he was not sure what he was going to do. More accurately, he knew what was going to be done but he did not know how it would be accomplished. He was prepared to rape her, or more aptly to vanquish her. Certain he was that there would be no salvation without total subjection, complete dominance. Exertion of his mastery over her would prove to himself that he was a total man, a propelling power, and a prime mover. More than a female, Estelle was the vessel into which he must pour out his frustrations and failures. Conquer her, and he might still have faith in himself.

The alcoholic liquid slithered down her throat leaving a warm sensation in its wake. Relaxed and yet eager for the appearance of the object of her mind's attention, she was barely aware that Dr. Mington had sat down beside her. She was totally unprepared for what was about to happen, and even later when she was to reflect back on it she was not sure that with any degree of awareness she would have acted any differently. Her drink went tumbling down to the floor as she was roughly pushed back on the bed. Damp lips pressed against her own lips. A gruff hand groped under her sweater for a naked breast. Hot, liquor-laden breath swept her face. A knee pushed her skirt up around her waist. An animalistic groan sounded in her ears as an oppressive weight pushed her down, seemingly ever further down. Then, abruptly, an agonizing sobbing against her chest, accompanied by inaction.

Thwarted by some inner force in the rape attempt, all of his emotional composure fully broke down. The sobs came from deep within, echoing a great inner misery, as he lay upon her. Through all of this she had been silent. No screams, no verbal protestations. It was several moments before he realized that her arms were around him, comforting and soothing him.

There had been no time to be fully repulsed or to interpose any sort of defense. Even after fully realizing that Dr. Mington had intended to rape her, almost upon impulse she drew him nearer rather than pushing him away. In this brief span of time, she had seemed to experience a revelation of the deepest workings of a desperate human being. Knowing that she felt no love for Dr. Mington as a man, yet the love in her heart for an evident act of futility led her to reach out for him in what she could only reason as an attempt to fill an anguished human cry for help. With only the sounds of his sobbing filling the confines around her, she could not fully understand why she was doing what she was doing. She pulled her sweater up to her neck and cradled his head between her breasts.

When it was over, she felt nothing. No pleasure, no remorse, nothing. The fact that she had given her youthful body to the perspiring, panting, and aging form beside her might closely be associated with an act of charity, although she earnestly felt that nothing had been given. Perhaps, she owed it to him. A form of tribute to his wisdom and to his maturity in order to span the gap between mind and body. Yet, without any sort of passion or feeling. Not as she would have succumbed to Justin, to give every muscle and fiber into the act of love. Instead, an instantaneous and meaningless mechanical body function. A surrender to Dr. Mington's frustrated need. Perhaps, merely a delayed reaction to all that had been pent up inside. Rationalization for an unexplainable action, the giving of love when none is felt. Her shame overshadowed any possible redeeming feature of the action.

Dr. Mington was tired. He did not feel victorious or even satisfied. The smooth flawless skin had been enmeshed with his, and for an instant he had been thrilled with the object of his love. Yet, he was really no better off than he had been before. He had accomplished no assertion of his mastery. To the contrary, he had broken down and whimpered like a baby. When he regained his breath, he muttered hoarsely, "Why do you pity me so much?"

It was an awkward moment before she responded. "I don't pity you."

Agitated, he shot out at her, "Then why did you do it?"

"I don't know," she whispered. "I really don't know."

As if confession would cleanse his being, he blurted out all of his feelings about her. He even told her every morbid detail of his family life, and how he had enticed her here on a ruse. After his last word was spoken, it just seemed as if he had summarized a classic case of failure and ineptitude. A portrait of an insignificant person.

Estelle listened without apparent reaction. She had let him make love to her, and evidently it had a great meaning for him. That she should let her body be used for such a purpose was against everything she as a female believed in. It was the staggering reality that she did not know why she did it that bothered her the most. The final proof that she totally lacked any understanding of herself, or any control over the events or course of her life. The abject hopelessness of it all swelled within her chest and she turned to him and wept as he enfolded his arms around her. Misconstruing her emotions, he felt uplifted at once. A glimmer of hope that his world might be righting itself.

TEN

The breeze ruffled the curtains causing the street lamp to flicker on the ceiling. It had been a long day, and he should have been exhausted, but at the moment he was luxuriating in the stimulation of relaxed attentiveness. For this one instant in time, he was at peace with the world and with himself. A tranquility that he coveted greatly. The new Justin Post would relish every facet of its grandeur.

The breathing of Kate Henderson was deep and steady as she slept by his side. He studied her form as best as he could in the darkness, enjoying the warmth and smoothness of her body where it made contact with his. She appeared to be a composite of so much human strength and solidness. In their growing intimate relationship, he had discovered no weakness of character or illogical crack in her philosophy. Her confidence was unshakable. Her perception and judgment keen and finite. Somehow, it all bothered him more than he thought it would or should. While her companionship and tenderness were what he needed most at this time, he was troubled by the larger picture. Not that he wished to shun a person because she was perfect, or at least possessive of all of the qualities of a person that he might ever deserve. Nor that he wanted or believed that a woman should in any way be inferior to a man. Yet, one of the lessons, one of the most painful insights that he had taken with him from the earlier experience with Rosalind, was that love may be protected by strength but is better fostered from the desire to aid weakness. One should not necessarily limit love or admiration merely to the person that can be looked up to. The human factor, the one imbued with all of the unpredictable facets of conduct and the frailest of perceptions, is really what sets us apart from one another. The crucial element of humanity in all of its infinite varieties. The vitality, the adventure, and the magic of rising to the top one moment, and then tripping or crashing downward the next, is the cohesion and challenge of the life form. The human factor, the one that can be loved the deepest.

Maybe, it was a form of self-delusion. He felt that he was good for Kate and that he did his share of the giving to their unison. He was not fully aware of her needs, if she had any, but their conversation and behavior had been sincere and honest. All had been natural and unforced. The greatest achievements may not be the ones heralded by others. The successful book, for example, might be an overt symbol of high attainment but its accomplishment merely superficial. It is in the matrix of the one-on-one relationship that true edifices are built, particularly between a man and a woman. Such a human construction project is not limited to one man and one woman. Even if he ever did find love again as he had with Rosalind, there would still be an assortment of emotional bridges to fill the human need. Perhaps, no one person can fill all of the wants of another in all circumstances. If that is so, one should not artificially deprive oneself of the opportunity, at least, of obtaining the greater emotional and/or intellectual fulfillment. Social barriers, even if transfixed as mores of the times, are the least sustainable artificial human confinement.

Try to reason about love and you will lose your reason [France].

Kate stirred in her sleep. Her hand rested on his arm, and the soft fingers pressed gently into his flesh. Her eyes were open, and she slowly drew his head down so that their lips were touching. After the kiss, she remarked rather business-like, "Those beautiful steaks are waiting in the kitchen. Meat and wine will be the crowning touch to a wonderful evening."

They ate in silence, not the quietness of hostility or boredom but the peacefulness of contentment. The wine blended with the easiness of the body, lulling them into the emotional tranquility of the here and now.

Staring into each other's eyes as they ate and sipped the wine, their souls communicated as if they were in full and complete discourse.

Her thoughts began to bother her. Somehow, she had the distinct impression that in spite of outward appearances she was not handling this situation very well. Struggling between fleeting youth and the gnawing unrest that accompanied her daily torment that life has to hold more for her than the day-to-day routine of teaching or being everyone else's role model, she did not want to lose this man. Marriage had never obsessed her. She had always been a natural and active participant in social activities. Her appearance and personality were nothing she needed to dwell upon. Either people accepted her or they did not, it was as simple as that. It was their problem and not her's. Somehow, beneath her austere exterior, she felt that when she was finally ready for marriage, there would be opportunities available. As the years filtered away, the dating exercise lost meaning and potential. Romantic desires became obscure and infrequent. With Justin, however, she felt a unique exuberance, a keen surge of the thrill of being alive and active. She could only attribute this to an emotional euphoria that she had held in abeyance for such a long time – love. If that is what it is, and she wished that it were so, she did not want to do anything that might jeopardize the current or long-term potential. Ready and willing to give up total independence and aloneness, she now wanted to share love's benefits and promise. It would be at its best with a man that she found so attractive. The problem that she had become aware of for some time, but which had become particularly troublesome only in the last few years, was that the more intelligence and academic experience she obtained, the smaller the circle of men became that drew her attention or raised the specter of compatibility. Justin was a man she could deeply respect. One who could and did match her physical and intellectual demands. The secret she knew so well at this point was not to let herself be governed by a developing state of frustrated desperateness, and to make sure that such was never revealed. The major difficulty rested in what form or manner to disguise it.

The bird chooses its tree, not the tree the bird [China].

"You seem far off," his voice interrupted her self-dialogue.

"Yes. Far off ..... and way out," she said rather hesitatingly.

"On your way out where?"

His humor touched her, and she smiled accordingly. "Out your way."

He matched her smile. "There has to be a better way than that!"

"You know that old expression, don't you? The person who judges himself has a fool for a judge."

"Ah! The poetic license of college professors. Dangled thoughts, mangled words. But, even if I judge myself... And I lose, can't I throw myself on the mercy of the court?"

"You could, and probably would. But, that would make you a two-time loser."

"How so?"

"Asking for mercy is a second negative. You have not won, but you ask for a tempering of the loser's fate. Better to face the full defeat and start anew."

"And, what if one bruises easily?"

"A human frailty that none of us can afford."

"A weakness, perhaps, but such a vital part of sensitivity and feeling."

The conversation had quickly turned more serious than she wanted it to, with hidden meanings. He seemed to be pressing it. She stepped back. "Maybe, I didn't express it quite correctly. I did not mean that one should not have that quality, but rather one should make sure that no one else should know that you have it."

"Are you speaking for yourself now, or just in general."

"Both."

"Are you afraid that others would know that you have feelings or what they might be?"

"I will adopt an old debater's technique and answer a question with a question. Do you think anybody else is capable of understanding my true feelings? I almost said care about my feelings, but that might be an overstatement."

Perhaps, he had found a soft spot in the rock. "Are you afraid to find out?"

"Are you psychoanalyzing me?" A little annoyance crept into her voice.

"No. I don't want to come across that way. But, we all have feelings. It is what makes us so human. What good is it if we harbor them within our-selves believing that no one else can take them for what they are, especially if another person is involved in the same set of facts or circumstances?"

"Aren't you assuming that feelings are capable of being expressed, that every facet of a person's being can be mouthed in oral communication?"

"No. Not at all. Most of the really meaningful expressions of one's feel-ings are revealed in other ways than the recital of words. When we make love, for example, or even just look at one another, to me, at least, we are truly communicating."

"Are we? Are we really? I don't know if I fully believe that. Sure, we are sharing an experience, a very pleasant one at that. But, does it really mean the same for you as it does for me? And, if you know the meaning that it has for you, and how many people take the time or trouble for such an introspection or can analyze at such a personal level, how can you relate or superimpose that feeling on me?"

"If two people share an experience, their frame of reference stems from the same overt act. Of course, while there is room for minor differences in perception, one has to believe that a common experience of meaning should serve as a bridge between them so that their sensual lives can cross and not let it act or intrude as a wall between such a potential joining. The few for-tunate ones touch in passing, no matter how briefly."

"An eloquent presentation, I admit. But, there are murky waters when one treads on eloquence. Generalities loom as particulars."

"Well, let's talk specifics."

She was silent for a moment. "I would rather not."

He looked deep into those dark brown eyes, and in a way felt a little relief at her apparent signal that this line of conversation had gone far enough. The last thing that he wanted was to let it get out of hand, and possibly lead to either of them saying something that might be too personally intimate. He liked the relationship simple and uncomplicated. His experience with half-baked commitments was too painful as it was.

> *The pleasure of love lasts but a moment.*
> *The pain of love lasts a lifetime* [France].

He spoke softly, "I am sorry. I didn't mean to press you. I guess I just saw myself too much in what you were saying. I am still a mystery to me, an enigma of sorts. Relating it to the larger picture, I am amazed how early in life people learn to hold things back. I see so much of it. I often become confused myself when I start to think that this might be the natural way. Yet, inside, I like to believe otherwise."

"You know the house rules. No wallowing in self pity here. The problems of the world were supposed to be left outside the door." She laughed, also inwardly relieved that the direction of the talk had changed. She was not clear as to what she wanted to do, but being embroiled in philosophical concepts was no solution for short or long-term goals. "How about helping me with the dishes?"

"I knew there would be a catch to all this. Why don't you wash, and I will show you exposition drying."

"Another ploy, I suppose."

"Right. We just leave them around after they are washed exposed to the air until they are dry."

"Good idea. But, to help me remember it in the future, let me try it now. You wash."

They hugged, cleared the table, and returned to pick up the pieces of their individually designed programs. Each, however, would dwell on what was said, especially on what might be read between the lines.

ELEVEN

Upon arising the next morning in his own apartment, Justin found a note that had been slipped under the door – *URGENT! I MUST SEE YOU TONIGHT. COFFEE SHOP TOO PUBLIC AND DANGEROUS. CAN I COME HERE AT 8:00? IF YES, WEAR A WHITE SHIRT TODAY. E.*

Slightly perplexed, he thought it had to do with some new sinister scheme being hatched against him by the students. Would victory be so short lived? Would he be able to muster up the fortitude and content to rise up over the heap again? Little did he realize that it had nothing to do with this, but in a white shirt he went to the University to confront another day, but at least without having to face the seminar. Tomorrow would be soon enough to present that renewed test of his endurance.

For Estelle, things were not that regimented. She had not slept at all, and even the early morning walk to slip the note under Justin's door had not helped her head or to calm her quaking interior. For years, she had been able to avoid emotional entanglements not of her choosing. Even the surrender to Ted was not a commitment as far as she was concerned. Now, however, without a single word to that effect having been spoken, she had a sinking feeling that she was irrevocably bound to Dr. Mington. A tragic intertwinement. It was much more than she wanted, a great deal more than she was ready for, and she felt utterly lost and confused. Justin was the only one she felt she could turn to, but she was discerning enough to know that it was based on a dual motive. While depending on him to help sort things out and to build up her confidence, she was also hoping that it would serve as an additional catalyst to bring them closer together. Yet, this was at great risk. The possible reaction could range from acceptance to rejection. She had no idea how he might react. An adverse reaction would devastate her even more than she was now. Her role as an ally was solidified, but their relationship, at least the relationship that she wanted, was fragile. It might only be fostered through positive means and not by a situation in which he might be forced to turn against his Department Head and become embroiled in the personal machinations of a distorted and bizarre situation. Everything in life was now intimidating. Why couldn't it all be predictable and effortless? Why does everything have to develop with so much pain?

From all of her readings, as a student of poetry, an involvement that had stayed with her over the years, she appropriately recalled these words of Samuel Ullman: *Youth is not a time of life; it is a state of mind. We grow old only by deserting our ideals. You are as young as your faith, as old as your doubt; as young as your self-confidence, as old as your fear; as young as your hope, as old as your despair.*

Tormented by uncertainty, it promised to be a long day before the appointed hour would arrive. She was only slightly bolstered when she saw his white shirt and detected the slight nod of his gentle face.

Wearing what she considered to be her most appealing outfit, she knocked at his door shortly after 8:00 o'clock. Her clenched fist trembled ever so slightly, and the knocking was timid and hesitant.

The door opened, and his smile immediately put her at ease. He was truly a beautiful person to her, radiating warmth and compassion. Her slenderness and alluring beauty were not lost on him either, and he sensed that there was going to be more at stake here than his merely being a listener. For any more, he was not emotionally prepared. For one who had crowded out emotions in favor of intellect as a form of penance, he was being exposed to too much too quickly. A form of emotional shock.

She walked past him as he closed the door. Settling on the sofa, she was not sure how to begin or exactly what she should say or how much to reveal. As if he recognized her struggle, and attempting to put her at ease, he said gently, "How about a glass of wine? I have some white wine in the refrigerator."

"I would like that."

Off he turned to the kitchen, using the break to his best advantage as well. In the recesses of his mind, the alarming thought struck him that this was not a position that a college professor should be in. Having a young and beautiful coed, one of his students, alone with him in his apartment could be a difficult situation to have to explain. Yet, it posed an uncompromising or not-so-innocent situation because that was the direction his own mind was turning to. Estelle was only Estelle, now at the center or core of his revolving fixation. The more that his thoughts attempted to drift from that center, the fuzzier things appeared to be. The more he became absorbed, the more he felt rootless. He was not sure where the present Estelle began and where the memory of Rosalind left off. Too many fresh reminders, too many undulations in the recesses of his mind. Too many tests of his will power one after another. The vulnerability paramount.

Sitting next to her on the sofa, they both sipped the wine in an uneasy silence, alternating their gaze from one another to the liquid in the glasses. She placed her glass next to his on the coffee table, slumped back into the cushions, and wet her lips. "Strange, this thing called life." She began speaking as if stuck in some distant geophysical plane, yearning to draw near to the human fireside. "Now I know why it is merely a continuing set of trials and tribulations. When I was home this summer, I looked forward to further growing this year. I thought, rather foolishly, that it would be exciting and fulfilling. Now that I have been forced to do that maturing in a much shorter and distressing period of time, I have made an important and depressing discovery. Growing is accompanied by aging, and the more one knows about life and the more confident one feels about facing up to it and conquering it, a certain deterioration takes place. Often imperceptible, that loss is difficult to adjust to. The energy wanes, and at times prevents the meeting of challenges. Most frightening, each failure has a cumulative effect. Each failure weighs oppressively heavier on an already sagging ego. But, I do see one thing clearly. I cannot go on alone. I need help. I am not so proud as to refrain from crying out. It is this form of self-honesty that is probably at the root of my problems. It is also what has brought me here tonight. Funny, I never thought in terms of emotional honesty in the abstract before, and maybe that is another valuable lesson that I have learned from all of this. Of course, I do not fully understand it. Yet, that honesty was always a preoccupation with me. When I was ten years old, I had a favorite pair of worn out jeans. One day, I saw a woman accidentally drop a five-dollar bill from her bag. I didn't yell to her, and when she left I picked up the money convinced it was good luck for me. I changed it into small coins so that I could drag out spending my treasure. For many months I carried the change around in the pockets of those jeans, as I spent little bits at a time. By the time I spent it all, I had holes in the pocket. Shortly after that my father gave me ten dollars. Without thinking, I put it in my pocket to savor later. It fell through one of the holes, and I lost it. To keep five, somehow I had lost ten. The moral was not lost on me. A silly lesson you might say, but it had a profound effect on me. Now, somehow, I find myself in much the same situation. It is not money this time. It is my emotions. And, I am terribly scared of them...and of me."

The thoughts streaked through his mind as he listened. Memories of times when he would sit with Rosalind for hour after hour, listening to the torrid explanations of her every thought and reaction that she could not help but share with him. He was, perhaps, merely a time machine, rushing to meet his past. Travel most likely on a collision course.

He reached out and touched her bare arm gently. She covered his hand with her own. It was all the impetus she needed to continue her discourse. "I don't know where to turn to next. For a moment, I thought of going home. A place of safe and familiar surroundings. My parents are truly wonderful people. They would not fully follow the meaning of my plight, but the comforting would be there. Yet, that is no answer. I know this much. I cannot run away from myself. Then, I thought of you. We have already found we can trust each other. I think you will be able to see my situation clearer than I can. I would trust your judgment and cherish your advice. My only hesitation is that I do not want to add to your problems. You already have your hands full."

Looking into his eyes for an answer, she glimpsed the encouragement before he actually spoke. "I have a feeling you think more of me than I am worthy of, or what I deserve. I don't know if I can begin to live up to your high expectation of me. But, we have shared some deep confidences, and that alone would prompt me to help you. If I can do so, I would very much like to be a portion of the high regard you have of me."

That was all the prompting that she needed to tell him everything. All of the details came tumbling out. All of the reactions precisely spelled out. As she drew near the end of her twisted story, once again some poignant words of a poem filled her mind. Lingering beauty in thoughts and dreams of long ago, ushering in present sequences. She could recall the words, but could not remember who wrote them.

> *So seize the moment*
> *While there is a moment yet to seize*
> *Take it now.*
> *Else faceless time*
> *Creep in on little cat's feet*
> *To take it.*
> *While I love you; while my love falls*
> *Like love shaken from a petal.*
> *Take me now.*

How and why it happened was not a surprise, but it warranted some deep introspection. Her eyes were closed, and the full lips were trembling slightly in the reliving of her ordeal. He raised her to her feet, leaned close and kissed the damp forehead. As gently as he could, he touched his lips to hers, stilling the quivering flesh. As he slowly withdrew, it was almost as if a new-found power seeped into his being. A force of staggering proportions, awesome in its immensity. All from a tender action. A personal element struggling for new life. He embraced her, holding her securely, and sensing confidently that his strength would be transmitted to her through the contact of their bodies. Warm and meaningful acts to subdue conflicts. Combined with fresh vigor and rejuvenated spirit, it consummates solidarity and seals pacts.

Moved by the propulsion of energizing heartbeats, the way lighted by an intense inner glow, clutched together in union they found a peace that they could mutually share to the fullest and believe together to the utmost. A shudder of sheer pleasure passed through them like a gigantic wave, and they drifted away on it, carrying them far away from the night and the despair. An unhurried pause in the rush of time.

Estelle was ecstatic. She just wanted to be held and loved. The warmth filled her to abundance. It radiated from within her, and he could sense the rising tide of emotion from the grip of her fingers and from that telling bodily contact. For her, this was the culmination as well as the beginning. Her painful period of insecurity and doubt had been magically lifted away. As for the things that she had been through which had appeared so overpowering a brief moment ago, now appeared insignificant in the light of this powerful awakening and discovery. After all, this could be no other than the love that she felt her life was destined for. The torrent of events had swept her into a whirlpool from which she had mercifully escaped into a serene haven. Outside dangers were now too remote to do her harm. This feeling of safeness and well being could be nothing else but love, a love deeper and more meaningful than she had ever dreamed possible for her to attain. She was at the crest of the highest form of a wave of human contentment. The most inspiring part was that it seemed as if the ascension was just commencing.

Justin was exhausted and justifiably confused. It seemed too big a task to try and keep all of the merging elements in his present existence separate in his mind's eye so that perspective and proportionality could be retained. The confusion of experience and experiment would not let that be. The similarity, or the wanting of similarity, between Estelle and Rosalind. To add to his state of helplessness, he was not sure whether he had gained or lost a key ingredient for his well being. He had grown confident towards mastering potentially menacing situations. Yet, he had the distinct impression that he was now drifting more than ever. Dangerously adrift on an uncharted sea, with the prospect of settling on any predeterminable place dimming. In an unchosen, unsolicited abbreviated period, his emotional life had become quite cluttered. While it served to release pent up emotions, in the last analysis it could only be an interplay between antagonists. At the moment, he was in love with three women – a ghost, a rock, and a flame. His immediate concern was Estelle. They had been swept up in a flurry of events ending in a romantic involvement. Apparently, this was what she wanted. But, did he?

He could not deny the physical attraction. She was so pretty, so appealing. Was the sensual environment also a product of his imagination? Whose tormented conscience was he really trying to soothe? What troubled him the most was that he was not functioning under normal conditions, either in atmosphere or personal circumstances. Could he stand such intensive involvement? Was it conducive to fostering true feelings or only wished for events? Yet, how could he deny the effects of the pressure of her embrace, the wholesome enthusiasm of the kisses on his neck, the soft touch of her skin? That reality was omnipresent. It could not be dismissed or ignored.

He guided her back to the sofa. "Estelle, I don't know if this is right or sensible. I suppose it is because we wanted it to happen. An enacted dream, if you will."

Gently caressing his cheek with the tips of her fingers, she whispered, "I don't know where reality ends and dreams begin. But, at this moment I don't care. Right now all of my life is in this one spot. Here, with you."

He smiled. "I have always been a dreamer. Dreams have always been more exciting and interesting than life. Anybody can become or attain the epitome of the most cherished dream. The quest should be made, even if doomed to failure. It seems like such a simple and logical conclusion. Only by setting one's goals and aspirations as high as possible can one achieve the highest of potentials. If people believe that they can be happy or perfect, they can get close to those ideals. There will always be something to strive for. Otherwise, self-motivation is thwarted. I don't mean to be talking in riddles, but we really know so little of each other."

She looked at him quizzically. "I have a feeling you are trying to tell me something, something that I am sure I don't want to hear. Otherwise, you are making a thing of simple beauty more difficult to comprehend than is necessary."

"Yes. I am trying to tell you something. It is hard for me to say, and it will be hard for you to accept."

She hugged him closer. "What is so hard to know about love? Love is a super power. Just having you......... at least, I think I have you, has helped put everything else behind me. It is all a bad memory. It doesn't even bother me now. Is that what is upsetting you?"

"No, Estelle." He broke from her embrace but reached for her hand. Their fingers entwined comfortably. "It is just that I, in a sense, have a past of my own. A past I would rather forget, but which I dare not remember. I learned that an individual can and should have a dream of his own, but that when he meets another and loves her, that dream, or at least a part of it, melds with hers. Together, that new combined dream should transport them to new heights. I don't know, frankly, whether I am capable of handling two dreams at once."

"Justin, you forget one thing. The one lesson I just learned so well. You do not dream alone when you are in love. If one person can build to the mountaintop, two can build to the stars. I sense that now. I feel such a power. I believe in it with every fiber of my body and mind. A foolish youthful delusion perhaps. But, the love I feel for you is as mature as time itself. We have already stood together against a nearly uncontrollable world, and we have tamed it. There should be no limit beyond that. As you have just pronounced. That has to be the goal we set our sights on."

She was elated with the genesis of her thoughts. Yes, she was confident now that all would be better, much better. She had truly overcome the last hurdle. Her life had turned in a new, brighter direction. Let Justin call it what he may, this was the reality she needed and wanted. Once again, she was in control and forward looking.

For Justin, things were not so uplifting. He knew that he had phrased his thoughts poorly. How could he tell her that it was not really the fear of handling two dreams at one time so much as that he had not yet lost an earlier dream that had nearly destroyed him? That threat still lurked in the shadows. The temptation to call her Rosalind was all the indication he needed to know that things were not so clear. Swept up by Estelle's story and the boundless limits of his own imagination, he had a premonition that he was in a situation that was going to be dangerous. His intellect of the present and his haunts of the past presented one cogent message – he could not proceed with any deep relationship until he had mastered himself. This lack of mastery had ruined his earlier attempts at involvement, and had left him disoriented and with a dangling ego. His dream machine was rusty. At the moment, the stars looked too far away for him to reach.

TWELVE

As soon as Justin entered the room, he knew things would be different. The students were already in their seats, except for one of them. Ted Amherst stood at the window, facing the door. A lectern was placed before him, and the desk moved to face that arrangement. A marked position for a debate, of that he was certain.

Written in bold letters on the blackboard:

PORT HURON STATEMENT OF THE STUDENTS FOR A DEMOCRATIC SOCIETY: "MEN HAVE UNREALIZED POTENTIAL FOR SELF-CULTIVATION, SELF-DIRECTION, SELF-UNDERSTANDING, AND CREATIVITY . . .

BLANTYRE CREED — INDOCTRINATION, CAPTURE THE MIND AND STIFLE THE SPIRIT, MAKE THE PEOPLE WEAK OF MIND AND DEVOID OF FEELING.

A quick glance around the room revealed that Estelle was not there. Puzzled by her absence, he knew that he had to leave all thoughts of his personal life behind him. This confrontation was going to be difficult enough with all of his faculties directed towards this involvement. A mental duel was in the offing, with the student probably well prepared to vindicate any earlier apprehensions of defeat. However, such assaults were Justin's intellectual battlegrounds of life, and the blood quickened its pace in his veins as he anticipated the fray.

"Professor Post." Ted bellowed the words out in prolonged fashion. "Today, we are going to have a debate. A trial of sorts. You and I are adversaries. The jurors are already in place. Since you had the opening and closing remarks the last time we met, this time I will go first. I will also have the closing statement, if that is necessary. I doubt that any retort will be required. The facts and the truth can prompt no contrary assertions. Our dialogue will represent serious consequences because you represent not only yourself but also the college bureaucracy, and should also hearken to the diametrically opposed societal conscience. I stand and speak for the rest of the world at large .... or, I should properly say, at small."

Justin recognized that this kind of interchange could provoke high emotions and misunderstandings. He had to handle it properly. To spark, without inciting. To kindle, without burning out of control. It was imperative that he set the manner and tone for the forthcoming drama. "We have already resolved that for the life and substance of this seminar there will be no teacher, no leader. We are all students, bound in the yet undetermined direction of our thoughts and knowledge. None of us knows it all. None of us can say with any degree of certainty that anything or everything we know is worth knowing, or even repeating. Even if it is worth knowing, the possible uses of that knowledge are probably so numerous as to commence a new dilemma. E. Armand has said so aptly that life as experience *abandons the city of Things Gained, goes out from the gate of Things Judged, and wanders toward adventures in the open field of the Unforeseen.* So, in the spirit of the unquenchable thirst for insight, I accept any intellectual challenge." With that, he sat in the chair at the desk and stared at Ted intently.

Ted played a moment of silence to its best advantage. A prelude to his forthcoming masterpiece. A piercing glance at each individual in the room, demanding strict attention. He proceeded, exuding the confidence his posture bestowed on him. "Steinbeck wrote: *I believe that there is only one story in the world and only one. Human beings are caught – in their lives, in their hungers and ambitions, in their avarice and cruelty, and in their kindness and generosity, too – in a net of good and evil. A man, after he has brushed off the dust and chips of his life, will have left only the hard, clean question: Was it good or evil? Have I done well or ill?* But, only a free spirit has a chance to choose with the full potential of success. Only a free spirit is not inhibited by the duress, subtle and overt, of a society which is ever intent on constricting the opportunities to do well. Without a say in the shaping of one's life, one falls victim to the existing social engineering and the brain drain of the mass media, the stultification of prescribed education, the false grandeur of suburban affluence, and the teachings or preaching of the entrenched bureaucrats. The fat cats have their day and beyond that as well."

A pause accentuated his continued oratory. "Government is no friend of the little people. It keeps members of society at war with and between themselves. It protects and perpetuates the special interests, the few who, under the guise of caring, are only out for the narrow prospects of their vested positions. Thus, the human element has no chance for true cohesion. Fragmentation takes on the appearance of normality. By being splintered, the people are weak and easily coerced. Law confuses the situation and makes it worse. Law does not, in fact, create or regulate order. It merely serves and protects those who are in power. Any salvation for this spirit of humanity to combat the brutal and unjust dictates of the stagnant elite rests with the development, the nurturing of a new outlook. The birth and cogeneration of a fresh philosophy. The young shall break the restrictive pattern. We will tear off the shackles of pre-ordained knowledge and behavioral patterns. In a new direction, a new and more just order will gestate. When we tear down the structures and false facades that surround us, literally and figuratively if need be, that keep us channeled and penned in to the pre-arranged formats, not only will ideas, customs, laws, and dictated reactions change, but drastic life images and styles will be altered in this inevitable transformation. Liberty and individualism will not be the hollow sounding visions that they are today. Society will be truly modernized and not obfuscated by sexy sounding phrases to appeal to the notion that change is going on all around us when in actuality the stagnation of inertia is prevalent. Our regimented world is antiquated. It has all but eliminated the vital aspects of human nature. How can one think if limitations are put on the very thought processes themselves? How can one feel when the preoccupation of the world around us is to subjugate true feelings and give way to the societal mores pre-approved for prescribed behavioral patterns? How can one act when the mechanism of natural action carries with it obligations or even sanctions? Perplexing in its bewildering simplicity, how can one love when being loved is tantamount to weakness and perversion? The practice of love should be a major part of the educational system. The love for the one or the many must be an essential aspect of growing into a functioning and productive adult human being. The multitude of violent reactions would then be secondary to the primary driving force of every day life."

Moving from behind the lectern and standing directly in front of Justin, Ted raised his voice to match the crescendo of his thoughts. " So, if one thinks or espouses theories in terms of love, solidarity, and justice, and that can be called anarchism, then I say that anarchism is a beautiful philosophy to be sought after and revered. We should shout it from the roof tops, echo it in the valleys. If it is anarchism in its purest form to combat cruelty, corruption, castration of the human spirit, and exploitation by the state, we readily embrace the anarchist banner. You may call us anarchists supreme! Then you will have no one to blame but yourself. For anarchism springs up only when a society is immoral or it restrains human rights. We believe in free development, in mind and body. The pursuit of a person's pure spirit. If we are anarchists, we are the ones so well described by George Bernard Shaw. We distrust state action and are jealous advocates of the individual. We wage desperate, thorough, uncompromising, and implacable war on all existing and future injustices."

Ted ceased his oration, glanced around the room, relishing the looks of admiration sent his way. He would say no more this day. The gates of controversy were now open, and he was hoping that this upstart young scholar would fall into the trap so neatly laid. After all, there was nothing that could rightfully be said to counter these premises. Carefully, he had chosen the obvious principles of a reasoned and caring outlook. If the creed were attacked, it would only add greater conviction to its fundamentals. The young would save the world from itself........and for them.

Justin was pensive, and he felt an inner controversy arise. This could no longer be a totally intellectual situation. Emotion was too prevalent, not only in the audience of sheep but in what he felt himself. There was just too much that Ted had alluded to that he believed in himself and wanted to continue to believe in. What were those words of Yevtushenko that he had read recently? Yes, he remembered them, and they appeared with a slow, tantalizing magic before his mind's eye.

> *Telling lies to the young is wrong.*
> *Proving to them that lies are true is wrong.*
> *Telling them that God's in his heaven*
> *And all's well with the world is wrong.*
> *The young know what you mean. The young are people.*
> *Tell them the difficulties can't be counted,*
> *And let them see not only what will be*
> *But see with clarity these present times.*
> *Say obstacles exist they must encounter.*
> *Sorrow happens, hardship happens.*
> *The hell with it. Who never knew*
> *The price of happiness will not be happy.*
> *Forgive no error you recognize.*
> *It will repeat itself, increase,*
> *And afterwards our pupils*
> *Will not forgive in us what we forgave.*

Justin rose to his feet. He scanned the faces in the room, longing to rest his eyes on Estelle's friendly presence. In its absence, he resolutely turned to Ted, nodded his head slightly, and turned to the student body. For an instant, he had an image of a sea of wheat blowing together in the wind. He began the arduous mental journey, not sure where this new road would take him and what might be found along the way. "Euripides said it well. *In pursuing great things, you may miss things close at hand.* Eliot said it in another way:

> *And the end of all exploring*

Will be to arrive where we started
And know the place for the first time".

He paused. The silence among the shafts of wheat was both inviting and frightening. "I know that each of you looks upon me as an outsider, as a representative of the Establishment that you feel suffocates you, and is to blame for all of the miserable conditions that you believe can be so easily righted. If only it were as simple as all that! The problem, though, is not one unique to your generation. It exists in various forms and nuances for all of us, for all ages. You like to think that the elders of society are all alike, duplicated robots of the dastardly world, and the beasts of a defiled nature. You are convinced that their only role or purpose is to perpetuate the institutions that keep your minds and spirit so contained that your socialization is rigidly channeled. It is all merely a matter of perspective. It is the common struggles that bind the members of each and every generation together. However, it should transcend that level to bind all of us intergenerationally. You are all students, with much in common. Your mutual struggle is to breach the educational obstacle course so that you can obtain the credentials to ease the struggle of having to find a job to make a living to support yourselves and your loved ones. That was, and still is, the same struggle of the generation that preceded yours, and the one before that. On and on, although the degree and circumstances may be so different that only close inspection can root out the similar base. It is just that the generation before you is one step ahead in meeting that demanding goal of obtaining financial security. The generation behind you will also face that taskmaster. The same tortuous path must be followed. It will look to them as it does to you, that nobody has bothered to put up signposts or warning signs. And for what, really? If one is lucky, and the so-called prime years are weathered and endured, you get to pursue a few pleasures to salve the decaying flesh and withering mind. Our senior citizens are involved in just that struggle. For all intents and purposes, they go it alone. Yet, each succeeding generation will reach that juncture. To achieve the dignity that maturity is supposed to bring along with it, while constantly fighting the disdain of others who look upon them as useless and treat them rudely. A very dismal picture indeed, but dismal only as an intellectual and emotional exercise because each one of us need not let this become our outlook or scheme of events. In the final analysis, it is not your generation that needs to be set free. It is all generations. The enemy is really all of us who compartmentalize society by distinctions such as age. While we should all strive to make our way of life better, society more responsive to all needs, and the world safer and at peace, the first battle is with ourselves. While it seems implausible to you, the elders were young once too. They also engaged in dreaming and high expectations. For many of them, as will be for most of you, that was left behind in the actual adventure of existence. For life, first and foremost, is an individual struggle. The fight to stay alive, to be free from hunger, and to be warm and safe. To exude confidence in actions and activities, to experience the receiving and giving of affection, and to bask in the glow of being needed. Such struggles change our perception. The list of needs becomes the category of wants. While the line between needs and wants is fuzzy, focusing on the actual distinctions may be crucial. Perhaps I am talking in circles. What I am trying to say is that I am not opposed to your objectives. They are not new or outlandish. Who can deny their basic validity? I cannot argue against their justness. Many of your parents and others have confronted the same crossing point in the journey to humanity. We only differ as to the means avowed to achieve change. Method is the true bone of contention. The direction and implementation of a plan for human goals, individually or collectively, is vital if we realistically hope to attain some degree of success with those plans. It is weak to generalize that the ends justify the means of getting there."

He cleared his throat, purposely pausing before beginning again. "Let me tell you two stories. Each involves a different childhood friend of mine. Each finds personal vindication to an internal conflict. Each one able to build upon that introspective enlightenment which in some small way attempts to make this a better world. The first story involves a young woman. This woman's strength of character, her will and determination allowed her to shun any preordained role for a woman in society, and to lead her to be the maker of her own destiny. This, long before women's liberation came to the forefront. Her family, discounting her possibilities in life solely because she was a female, forced her into becoming a teacher, even though she was exceptionally gifted and otherwise inclined. Her determination, fighting against great odds and constant rebuke, with personal sacrifices often bitter and hard to bear, detaching herself from the disapproval of her family and so-called friends, she went to law school. Taking evening classes because she had a menial job during the day, she graduated in the top ten percent of her class. She has since gone on to a brilliant career in the law, shunning a remunerative practice offered to her male contemporaries, to practice what is now known as public interest law. Representing the downtrodden, the unfortunates forsaken by facts and circumstances, she has become a true champion of unpopular causes. A public protectorate. Overcoming all of the adversities thrust in her way, she has met a noble life's goal. Approval by her peers and superiors was never solicited or important. Personal courage to set a course so that she might have the where-with-all to right a wrong that most others would not tackle. I sleep better at night knowing that people such as she are out there. As with conscientious journalists, they are the true watchdogs of our society. In the law, she has found a personal satisfaction. She uses a tool that society has developed and offered against itself as a vehicle to make things better. Combating injustice and inequality is her success. A personal aspiration that leads to a high public purpose. In the right hands, the law can be a powerful weapon as well as a shield. Contrary to the opinion of the law that you heard expressed earlier, she has found the significance in the words of Cicero – *we have bound ourselves to the law so that we may be free.*"

His throat was parched, but he dared not break the momentum of the moment. "The second story involves a young man, shy and reserved. He always had difficulty in talking with others, but I remember even from the earliest days he had a flare for writing. I was fortunate enough to be part of his growing years. He has emerged as one of our nation's most talented young novelists. But, it was what he was to do with that great ability that is worth relating here. He developed an introvertish activity into a worldly offering. Not only the beauty of his prose, but the enlightenment of his ideas are immortalized for all time and available to all those who wish to dwell upon them. He has taken it upon himself to institute inner city writing clinics, a type of outreach program where he combines the joys of writing and reading so that expression can be focused in creative ways. Communication can be free flowing. In a sense, he has turned his personal and individual achievement into a gain for all of us. He enjoys the sense of giving by sharing his gift with others so that they too can find some fulfillment by phrasing their own thoughts into text. The fruits of the harvest for them to savor. A small advancement in a setting which does not prompt personal success. Perhaps, in small measure, but a beneficial effect and model for society at large."

Another pause, another emphatic lesson to bestow. "What is the moral of all of this? Society is merely a collection of individuals. It is as strong and as flexible as those components are at any given moment. While it is worthwhile that we are all thinking and feeling for the common good, that we attempt through concern and mutual action to right the wrongs on the local, national and world levels, we should never lose sight of the fact that we, all of us, have a set of special inner needs that require satisfying, either apart or in conjunction with those larger struggles. There is a niche in this life for each of us. It is our own special emotional and intellectual place. A snug harbor. For your own contentment, for the confidence that is so necessary to persevere in an often uncivil life containing numerous hardships and disappointments, it is vital that you seek for and find that personal haven. This may sound like preaching to you. I certainly don't mean for it to sound that way. Yet, I am trying to create an atmosphere here for a limitless intellectual exercise. We must all concede, myself included, that there is much room for exploration and growth. I encourage each of you to speak as freely as you can or want to. As you might converse one-on-one with your closest friend. Express whatever sentiments you would like, no matter how antagonistic or disquieting they may be. To dispel your antipathy to the college world, independent thinking is paramount here. Each to be his or her own person. Discard all of the pre-existing patterns, those of your elders as well as your peers, and work through each idea or set of concepts on your own. Reach a conclusion that feels right for you. You will be better off for that, and it will rub off on the world around you. You will be at that moment who you are and not what you think others want you to be. You need not prove anything to anybody but to yourself. When all is said and done, isn't that what really matters? Isn't that the most logical starting point for tackling your world?"

The silence was pervasive. Justin picked up his papers and left the room before the period had ended. His words hopefully would register in the young minds and settle in the collective quiet. The impact was great upon himself. After all, it was his reason for being here. This too was the agony that drove him towards despair. This too was the quest that preoccupied him and threatened to consume him. That the words were spoken was important. Now, he had to listen to them himself.

THIRTEEN

Ted was oblivious to his surroundings. The effects of the intellectual exchange were not what he had intended or desired. Yet, it was not without a great deal of substance for him. Perhaps, he was not quite the radical he had held himself out to be. He not only listened to what had been said, but he also liked the man who had said it. Here, at last, was the first person he had ever come in contact with from an older generation that he was able to admire. It surprised him to the point that it represented a shock to his system, a jolt to his psyche. He also realized that discourse and debate could be a very potent means of settling or unsettling a turn of events.

It all gave him his first glimpse into what he had succeeded in avoiding before, thinking about his own future. Rarely had he thought of himself in any long-term plan. The here and now was always the paramount interest and concern. That concentration had totally preoccupied him, completely satisfied his reason for being. Now, however, he had the initial and exciting expectancy that at some tomorrow he would like to be doing and to accomplish what this different kind of man had just displayed. In an academic environment, he would like to prod, inform, guide, and tease the mental faculties of young, growing minds. He could never abandon fighting the system. There was just too much wrong with it. Yet, college need not be the matter of expediency as much as the object of expectancy. Such a revelation was at the same time both baffling and illuminating.

He was now alone in the classroom, and it was a new source of comfort for him. While he had exalted in the presence of crowds, eagerly seeking attention and approval, he suddenly realized that this was not what he was most happy with. It was not what Estelle had been satisfied with, and perhaps in her silent ways and recent outbursts such was the wisdom she was trying to convey to him. Right now, it did not matter what the other students thought of him. Leadership had been so alluring. Now, a new perspective on himself and about his surroundings had taken over. In honesty to his own creed he had to confront it, to admit it to the entire world if necessary. The man had been right when he said that one must also make a commitment to oneself.

When he did leave this comforting posture, even the campus appeared to have new grandeur. It instilled a feeling of worthwhile pride in him, and he found himself impressed by it for the first time. It was almost as if he was seeing the surroundings so that a complete picture revealed itself for him to absorb. Wouldn't Estelle be shocked by the nature of this revelation?

For Estelle, the turn of events that day was not so comforting. She had not intended to miss the seminar. Brain and heart drew her to be part of that occurrence. Yet, she could not foresee Dr. Mington waiting for her in his car along the way, and the desperate and pathetic plea that she drive with him a short distance away so that he might bare his soul. He described this in heart-rending terms as the ultimate degradation.

Parked in a remote area close to the campus, she sat rigidly with her side pressed against the door. He, in silence, hunched over the steering wheel. His clothes were unkempt, his hair and beard unruly. The puffed hands trembled visually. It seemed improbable that this same man was the mental giant that she had once held in such high regard. But, that was at an earlier period, a lifetime away. At this instant, perplexed and floundering, she had nothing to say. There was a complete absence of feeling or emotion. Above all, she was disappointed and mystified at her own agreement to be there or anywhere with him.

When he began to speak, it was not the resonant, confident voice she had always associated with her mentor. "Estelle, in a very short time, I have learned more about myself and about life than all of the experience and book knowledge accumulated over the years. It has been a disturbing insight. It is no secret to you. After all, you are involved in it as much as I am. Maybe, even more so. You are to blame for what I have become." He stopped long enough to confirm his feeling that she would not interrupt him or challenge these brash assertions. "And, what is crucial, you are solely responsible for what will happen to me from here on out."

He could not help but feel inwardly pleased with himself. She was really not the fault or cause of his predicament. He knew that. But, he had convinced himself that she represented the catalyst for the actual physical and mental deterioration. After all, he had gone on for years languishing in a discontented situation but at least one that had posed no immediate threat to all he had. Now, everything had changed. His home life was shattered. He would not be able to face or handle the responsibility and demands of his position at the University. With such a grim picture, it was only just and proper that she should share the blame for his downfall and be obligated to make it up to him.

"I have no family, no home, no job," he lamented. "All given up for you. That is my sacrifice. What are you going to do about it? What are you going to do for me?"

Facing her, his beady and blurred eyes pierced the thin cover of her composure. Yet, once again he was unable to perceive her reaction. She, as well, was unable to control what was about to happen. Gripped by a strange form of mental terror, an emotion that entrapped her with merciless determination, an unfamiliar part of her character emerged in possessive dimensions. Anger crept from her insides to the mouth, the lips forming a torrent of dramatic words in a high, fervent pitch. "You arrogant, stupid oaf! You are not going to lay that guilt trip on me. Whatever you are, whatever you did to yourself and to me you did by yourself and because of yourself. I am not to blame here. I will not admit or accept that kind of sick responsibility. You took advantage of me. You abused me and the trust I had in you. I hate myself for letting you do that to me. But, not merely as much as I hate you for doing what you did. I respected you. I admired your intellect and worldliness. You were my idol. You violated that relationship. Can you understand that? Now, I utterly detest you. The disillusionment hurts me the most. I owe you nothing, absolutely nothing. You already got from me far more than you ever deserved. I will never give you anything again. I will never have anything to do with you. You are a complete, degraded louse. Mean and despicable."

With that surge of epithets, she threw open the car door and stepped out. "You leave me alone, or I will call the police and tell them everything." She slammed the door, running off in the direction of the campus. The cool breeze touched her flushed cheeks, and she ran as fast as she was able. Each step carrying her further away from an upsetting segment of her life.

He sat there stunned. This was not what he had expected or planned on. Sure that he had her within his grasp, the scheme seemed sure to succeed. What he had so carefully devised was now in ruptured turmoil. Now, she was gone. It did not seem that he would ever get her to be with him again. He had nothing left at all. The abject condition engulfed his being and consumed his threadbare spirit. The self-pity swelled within his chest and he could feel the tears roll carelessly down his cheeks. That was all that he could feel.

FOURTEEN

Back in his apartment, Justin's exhaustion replaced the earlier exhilaration of gaining an upper hand over the students. Victory and his own personal plight slid into the background as his eyes closed. Sprawled across the bed, he basked in the momentary physical comfort and slithered into a deep sleep. How long he was asleep he did not know, but the frantic knocking at the door awoke him abruptly.

Opening the door, it was the last person he expected to see. It was not the Dr. Mington he had known. His personal appearance was a shamble, his frame stooped and seemingly sapped of the dignity that had once been so evident. The warmth in the eyes extinguished. A vision akin to a form of walking death. Perhaps, merely a ghostly apparition after all.

The two men stood facing each other without speaking. Justin was frozen with indecision. He could neither bring himself to strike out at him nor to invite him in. Dr. Mington was the first to speak, a voice devoid of resonance and life. "I know I don't deserve this, but I have to talk to you. May I come in?"

Without replying, Justin ushered him in. Sitting at the kitchen table, Dr. Mington cleared his throat. "May I trouble you for a glass of water. Then, I have a long, rather complicated story to tell you. But, I don't have the energy to tell it, and I doubt you would have the patience to listen to it. I will just tell you the upshot of it all."

With the glass of water partially drained, he continued in a voice barely audible. "I don't blame you or Estelle for hating me. Apparently, that is the only emotion I can raise in people. I certainly don't think highly of myself either. But, before I leave all of this behind me, please hear me out." After a pensive moment, he continued in a weary drawl. "I imagine that my philosophy is as unrealistic as I am. Any way, it doesn't seem to matter at this point. Whether it makes any overt sense or not, one does not have to know where one is going until he actually stops. The movement obliterates the destination. I have now, thanks to Estelle, stopped running. She has supplied a violent upheaval of my being, and perhaps for the first time in a long while I have the courage to face myself. I have created a total disaster all around me. My family connection is ruined, and teaching has held nothing for me for years, far longer than I care to remember or think about. Rather than focusing on myself, I used Estelle, first merely the thought of her, and then the actual being, as the cause of .... or, perhaps, the solution for .... my misery. Anything but to have to confront the real me. Estelle said some pointed things to me this morning, and as disturbing as her reaction was, I know she was right. I am truly sorry for what I did to her. She does not deserve the additional weighty burden I heaped on her. But, just as I know I cannot ever face her again, to try to explain or to apologize, these are my failures and not hers. They are beyond redemption. Over the past hours, my thinking has led me to a clear decision. I must leave here, leave all that this place represents. Only away from here, away from the actual reminders of my failures, my weaknesses, do I stand a chance of putting myself back together again. I do not know where I will go, and the place is probably unimportant. Wherever my meager funds will take me, there I will rebuild my crushed spirit. I leave you as the shadow of what I once was, and only hope that there is some lesson for others to learn from my downfall. I regret that I let you down, let you all down." With bowed head and eyes cast sadly to the floor, a lifeless self-portrayal was on exhibition.

Justin truly did not know what to say, or even if he could find the words, how to utter them. Torn between sympathy for the expressed burdens and the repulsion fostered by the deeds done, he knew that when he found the words to say that they would be non-committal and non-supportive. "Dr. Mington, of course only you can decide what you must do. From my own experience, I know that it is very difficult to escape from the past, no matter the distance effectuated. I have learned some important lessons in the brief time that I have been here. The teacher who stops learning relinquishes understanding. Perhaps, the most important thing that I have learned is that to know oneself is very difficult, a problem compounded by the deception of reality and the illusion of tomorrow. The students feel this the closest. I hope they don't shrug it off under the guise of youthful fancy. Little do they realize that they are doing more for me than I can ever do for them."

"The pity of it all is that some lessons come too late to right a bungled existence."

"Perhaps, not to turn back, but to turn ahead."

"Yes, I suppose I must work at that." Rising to his feet, Dr. Mington went for the door. Filtering ever so clearly into his mind were the words he had read a long time ago. Concepts that now came so prophetically in an emotionally charged vision. Words to the effect that all men feel love and hate, but old men know that both are filled with pain.

Turning, just before he passed beyond the door, he mumbled, "Some day you will all forgive me."

Justin watched the door close behind Dr. Mington. He stared after him, pondering long and deep insights into the varied ways of human behavior. How unpredictable such behavior can be, no matter how theory might dictate a prescribed reaction. Emotional transitions and dynamic personalities can cloud the outcome even more. Each a new case study to transcribe and mull over. Self-exploration can be joyous or painful. Little wonder that some people refuse to partake in such extrapolation, fearing the agony will be more than they can cope with. Living up to expectations casts a greater spell over the subject. It is an emotional exercise all must face at some point, or at many junctures. Once the initial hurdle is passed, the subtleties of human relationships can be recognized and experimented with, and a proper perspective gained to reach the maximum level of enrichment. How wide is the gap between learning and knowing! So much experience, so much insight for his unwritten book. A book whose intricacies he was now living. Would he ever find the time and energy to set it down on paper?

Another knock on the door broke his analytical discourse. Half-expecting

Dr. Mington with an after thought, a gentle relief was felt upon being greeted by Estelle's warm smile. Before he knew it, she was locked in his embrace. They kissed. Sensual. A poetic and surprisingly orderly and fitting human contact. Representing not only the passion of the moment, but also all of the yearnings and desires of young blood. Release for the pent-up emotions they both had been immersed in. The touch of lips, the sealing of an unspoken contract. The consideration of imparting mutual tenderness, ecstasy and warmth. Interdependence of the most basic and most powerful form.

Hand found hand, and as fingers entwined they walked to the bedroom. A fleeting moment in time, where, when the combination falls just right, one brushes elbows with infinity. To know as no one else can know who has not lived it. The flame flickering deep within, smoldering amidst the embers of their hearts until its effects spread to every part of their bodies. In a transport of delight they journeyed to every corner of the universe, lived every moment of history anew, and waded through the tides of eternity. The Earth seemingly stopped turning. Weightless, they floated to a kingdom of pleasure and beauty so immense and bountiful as to defy description by the world's greatest poets and painters. Yet, bodily they never moved from the bed. Brighter and warmer the flames grew, melting two hearts into one. The consolidation of two spirits. A joint enterprise of loving souls.

FIFTEEN

The day after the night before. A new and bright beginning, supposedly offering reflection and sobriety. Yet, for Justin the day brought no respite to his fractured sensibilities. Even with Estelle back at the dormitory, the solitude offered him little solace. Designed to further self, the reality of his plans had led him to a series of commitments to others. With Dr. Mington gone, his undertaking to and containment by the University seemed even more pronounced. His involvement with two women had him headed on a personal collision course. Events rather than design now guided his future. Today, at the least, he would lose himself for as long as possible at the University library to prepare for the next session of the seminar. Perhaps, where no one could find him, the pressures might ease. The perpetual dreamer lost in his dreams. The worst delusion of all delusions.

A library had always been an imposing symbol in his life. It promoted scholarship and satiated his love for books. It was a restful, peaceful place. A haven for an intellectual recluse. One could hide and get lost in some secluded corner. Books are powerful tools and their messages can capture and inspire the full range of human emotion and capability. The silent partners for all human endeavors. The cogent trial and error for thinkers and doers. If only the attainment of actual emotional growth and stability matched the pursuit of academic knowledge. If only common sense could be a subject to study and adapt to.

The library would only be a temporary refuge. Today, he had to resolve his social order. He was supposed to meet Estelle at an isolated spot off-campus for a picnic lunch, and he was expected at Kate's for dinner that evening.

Tomorrow was another seminar day, and he truly did not know what to expect. Estelle had informed him that she had heard nothing adverse or concerning ill plans for the forthcoming meeting. Yet, he did not anticipate that Ted would give up easily. The clash meant too much to him and for the ideals he pronounced. The intangibles were imponderable. Yet, they loomed large and possibly overbearing.

Estelle arrived at the picnic site before Justin, enabling her to once again bask in the gratifying euphoria encasing her very being. A mixture of excited expectancy and the calm of feeling the ultimate duality of caring and being cared for. Sensing for the first time on an adult life scale what she had only previously experienced as a child. A sensation running from deep within soothing all of her faculties. The well being not an isolated event but a component of a stronger and grander scheme. It filled her with new confidence, fresh perceptions, and an exuberance that she cherished. It sharpened the beauties of the day, kindled the fires of her revived inner spirit, and placed her in the land of the giants. No mere mortal could now disturb this haven.

When Justin appeared, their confrontation melded into an initial guarded expression of affection. As they settled silently down to the prepared sandwiches, an unusually warm autumn sun encased them. The rustling of the newly fallen leaves serenaded their culinary participation. The setting and their togetherness temporarily obliterated whatever trials and tribulations lay before them. For Justin, that meant that he could not tell her about Kate, or the anxiety of his situation. For Estelle, the yearning to discuss long-range relationships and commitments shifted into the comfort of the moment. It reinforced the feeling that had already been expounded upon. Their being together and sharing any given portion of time and space represented a magical exclusivity. It bolstered Estelle's capacity to love, and added a further serene confusion to Justin's outlook.

"Justin," she began in a gentle, melodic tone, "I am very happy."

He responded with a broad smile. "I share that pleasant feeling."

"Funny, really. I always thought that happiness was something I would want to shout out about, a triple rhyme to cap the gladness. I thought I would want to share it with others. But, I feel very selfish about it and about you. I can't even bring myself to tell my parents just yet."

Tightening his grip upon her hand, he asked softly, "And, if you did tell them, what objective facts would you present that might convince them that you were not crazy? How would you describe how you feel that would not conclude in their minds that you are laboring under a classic case of infatuation with one of your teachers? What might you say that they would believe as you do?"

Her eyes shifted to the trees, and her gaze was far off in the distance. "My parents are not like that. I would not have to convince them of anything. As long as I did not jolt the faith that they have in me, they would understand. At least they would try to understand. They probably would just accept it. They are wonderful people, and I can hardly wait for them to meet you. I appreciate them more now after experiencing the feelings I have for you. It all represents a kind of continuity. It is as if I have come full circle, and can meet them on another dimension."

"Unfortunately, I did not have such family sharing and involvement. For me, it was merely a surface relationship. I was forced to keep my personal struggles to myself. But, it was not the worst of turns. It forced me to build up a strong inner self. It gave me the ability to turn into myself and away from the world if the need arose. I could always hide within myself. There was always a place to regroup and fortify to meet outer struggles."

"I hope that neither one of us ever has to run or hide from anything any more. Together, we are invincible. I think the real reason I haven't told my parents yet is that I am not fully convinced that you are real and that this wonderful episode is happening to me, actually happening for me to hold. I don't use these words easily. I love you, Justin."

He grasped her hand with some urgency. In spite of his earlier hesitancy, he knew that he had to begin the unfolding of his life and weaknesses to her. Perhaps, it was too early to talk of Kate. That might right itself. He had to find a way to dispel the god-like image she had of him. "Estelle, I am the last person to want to daunt your emotional heights. I am a willing participant in the intimate involvement that lifts you so much. But, if we were to remove ourselves, step back, and look at this relationship objectively, it may not be all that it seems to be."

He did not have to wait too long to hear the disappointment prompted by his remark. "Justin, what are you trying to say?"

He was silent for a long moment. Convinced that he was being fair to her, he plunged ahead. "You and I have been subject to very unusual and fast-moving events. You have been through a trying emotional ordeal. I have been, and continue to be, tested for potential slaughter. I know we have not talked about this, but I am also susceptible to the after-reactions of an involved emotional event. Believe me, I am not telling you that I do not love you or that you do not love me, or that our feelings towards each other are not genuine. What I am trying to say, and probably not very well, is that there is a very fine line between what is and what we think we have. The needs we develop color perceptions and reactions, bringing them into a picture of the way we think things are and what we might like them to be."

Her eyes watered, a symptom of the twinge in her heart. "I hear your words but I can scarcely believe you are saying them. You are complicating the simplest of human behavior. I can't believe you mean them? What more can I trust than my own heart? It is the only honest command that I have. What I feel is wonderful. Why question it? Why risk losing it?"

"A fool I may be, but I am not questioning it in that sense. What I am attempting to convey to you is that this is not an uncontrollable situation. We can give it direction and even a greater purpose. We should question it. Others will. If we need to defend it, we must be prepared to justify it. Emotion coupled with events has set the design but we owe it to ourselves to analyze it. You should know me better. If our love is of superior strength and of lasting tolerance, forthcoming challenges will be handled with ease. First, we must know each other better, much better. A commitment only becomes irreversible when it is total."

"Justin," her voice showing some strain, "I don't know why you are saying these things. I also don't know what prompted you to say them. I can only interpret it as some uncertainty on your part, some doubt of how you feel towards me. I cannot deny that this hurts me because I have no hesitation in declaring my love for you, complete and forever."

Still gripping her hand with a firm tenderness, he whispered, "Believe me, I don't ever want to hurt you."

"As you say, I have been through much lately. Yet, I am deeply hurt. Perhaps, in part by my own disappointment. The nonfulfillment of what I feel to be a natural sequence of events. I suppose I should, if this were a movie, get up and walk away, leaving you to ponder the misfortune of your deeds. But, I will not walk away from you ever. I love you. I accept all that it involves. I have also learned from what has surrounded me, by my peers, by my mistakes, that even if I have to fight to keep that love intact, I will do it with all I am worth. Even if this fight is merely to rid you of any doubts you may have that this is real."

He sighed. "Estelle, I accept that challenge, and I hope sincerely that you prevail for both of our sakes. You are the best thing that has happened to me in a long time. But, I really do not believe any lack of effort or increased diligence on your part is what is important here. The problem, if there is one, or if I may call it that, rests with me. It is time I told you why I came here. It says more about me than even I can fathom."

Without the benefit of preplanning, the story unfolded. If he had contemplated its telling, it probably would not have been told with such honesty, although even the words could not fully convey the depth of its impact upon him. It may not have even fully apprised her of the extent of the challenge that it all represented. The facts were there. His only actual misjudgment might have been the extent of Estelle's capacity to handle it all.

Her reaction to his saga of Rosalind was a delightful surprise to her. There was no raging disappointment or jealousy. Not only did she feel that she understood what he was going through, but her maturing process let her put it all in its proper place for her to react to it calmly. For both of them, that was most necessary. She was astute enough to see that their individual struggles were not on opposite extremes, and that if her love for him were a solution for her, it would be the same for him. He need not worship a memory when she could supply all that it represented and more. She, for her part, could vanquish a memory. That she would be there in flesh and spirit, and she would make sure that she was, would be enough. That kind of confidence she had never shown before. Each new attribute of this deep felt emotion brought new rewards and added proof of the fulfillment of her quest. It was the confirmation of her new being.

As for the desire and struggle to write this new book, she could readily comprehend the compulsion to write it. She recognized and appreciated his intellect, and supported the philosophy that he espoused. She had much to learn about the intricacies of his beliefs and desires, and it was the sort of learning and participation that would further bind their love. Hopefully, she could inspire his task to fruition.

As they parted, they both felt better. Estelle basked in the additional discoveries of her adulthood. Justin was somewhat relieved that he had bared some of the inner turmoil, and was pleased by her acceptance of it all and the non-perplexity of her reaction. After all, her point was that maybe it was only threatening because he was letting it be that way. That was something that he wanted to believe. Yet, it is a fragile pulsating line that divides emotional victory from defeat. It is far easier to affix some permanence to such a line for the problems of others than for oneself.

Now that he was alone, he was not quite sure what he had accomplished. Especially when she would find out that there was at present yet another woman in the total picture. Not all anxiety can be shared. Not all agitation can be quieted. Not all truth is honesty.

SIXTEEN

When Kate greeted him at the door, his dilemma grew instantly. As they embraced, Justin could not deny the thrill her body gave him as it pressed towards him. The clean fragrance of her hair, and the smooth skin, all contributed to what he had known all along but was unwilling to face. While with Kate, he was in love with her. When with Estelle, that is where his love resided. There was no plausible way to explain it. Immersed in a conflict of his own making. Seemingly trapped the deeper he sank into it.

Love. What power that word held for him. It was distressing that it could be thrust on him so quickly and easily. An unwelcome intruder in otherwise orderly schemes. Amidst this total preoccupation with his own feelings, for an instant he saw himself with such clarity that he shivered with an overwhelming fear. He was afraid of himself. The pain of smoldering ashes of apprehension. The question really was not whether he was in love with two women at the same time but whether he had the capacity to love at all. Had he been a fake all of his life?

In that silent moment that he held Kate close, he looked at her with new circumspection. The short, straight brown hair clung to a well-formed head. A small, pointed nose symmetrically poised above thin lips. Not a beautiful woman, but certainly an interesting and expressive face accompanied by an appealing body. Intellect and wit lavished upon friend and foe alike. A bearing represented by refinement. Movements generated by confidence and promising hidden warmth. A natural smile, revealing nearly perfect teeth, connoting receptiveness. The fluidity of adjustability prominent in speech and body language.

For Kate, she luxuriated in the easiness of body and mind that she had rarely felt. Rarely had she been so relaxed with any person, man or woman. It was almost as if all her life had been preparatory for this involvement. The truly first relationship with a man that she apparently wanted to press on with more than he did. In fact, she knew that she would be impatient through the dinner in anticipation of the lovemaking beyond. In the concentric circles of her practical guiding principles, for once reason and opportunity were present at the same time. She sensed a new and very exciting emotional experience – desperate enrapture. Her strength of character would not help her if this relationship ended. If this were to be lost, she had a brooding sensation that disappointment would be great and loneliness even greater. More than adequate grounds for a reciprocating fervent embrace.

Not far away, another soul was contemplating another kind of loneliness. The abandonment of a cause. A transition in a fleeting moment of sempiternity. Ted Amherst trapped in the unexplainable dichotomy of things that never seem to change and those that never appear to be the same. But, this insight, this astoundingly simple personal revelation was really due more because of the presence of Justin Post. A kindred spirit. A wisdom seeker. A teacher as the mental prophet that he now aspired to become. The words of Hesse sprang to his mind: *He had thought more than other men, and in the matters of the intellect he had that calm objectivity, that certainty of thought and knowledge, such as only really intellectual men have, who have no axe to grind, who never wish to shine, or to talk others down, or to appear always in the right.*

Ted knew that to become a teacher he would somehow have to fit in with the established order. Even the so-called radicals on the faculty had made that kind of concession. Their freedom to teach and espouse ideas was tempered by the strictures of set programs and quantifiable elements. It would also mean a factional break from the leadership role he now enjoyed with the students. He doubted that any of them except Estelle would understand that. Perhaps he owed it in part to her as well.

This newfound experience and forward-looking idealism left him exhilarated. It filled him with hope, with strength, and with a new purpose. Two lines from a poem by Wilfred Owen seemed so appropriate as the slogan for the new Ted Amherst:

Courage was mine, and I had mystery,
Wisdom was mine, and I had mastery.

A thought brought a smile to his lips and a noticeable beat to his heart. A possible outcome might be the winning back of Estelle. He realized more than ever that she was the kind of woman that he needed and who deserved to be by his side.

Kate could not remember when she had felt so alive, so content. The nervous energy that had permeated much of her ordeals now appeared quite subdued. A greater force now overshadowed her commitment to ideals that had governed her existence. The most telling point was that she felt at ease with this delightful man, a man who displayed all of the loving movements and sensitivity that she craved.

"It is wonderful being with you, dear Justin." Her voice came from deep within her, almost as if it was trying to escape from a prolonged bondage.

His reply was measured. "I enjoy all we share. I also value your opinion, and I have a dilemma that I would welcome your advice about. As you know, I have this book inside of me bursting to be set free. I have had no time to work on it. The seminar demands so much of my attention and energy. Yet, it is as if it is my book. I seem to be living it. It is taking on a life of its own. On one hand, I feel uplifted by these developments. On the other hand, I am physically and emotionally drained. I feel as if I am having a dramatic and a substantial impact on the young minds, a goal that the book is to be designed to accomplish. Yet, I am no hero. If the truth were known, I am terribly afraid of the continuing confrontation even though it has been entirely a mental one. Basically, I am a writer. I am used to not having my audience right before me. Am I making any sense at all?"

As much as she would have preferred talking intimately on their personal involvement, she accepted his reaching out to her for counsel as a bonding mechanism. The further removal of barriers between minds to allow hearts to enjoy utmost freedom. "I don't think that there is any teacher worth his salt who has not been tested time and time again by mental challenges and agonizing demands on content and ethics. How many real chances do we get to mold those groping minds? Testing the capacity threatens the lifeline. At what point do we stop teaching and get involved with indoctrination? My principles are so entrenched that they often color my interpretation of facts. Yet, we know that the truth is ethereal. Perhaps, a teacher's greatest accomplishment can only be to undertake intellectual endeavors without worrying about where they may lead. There are degrees of truth. At times, more than one truth relates to the same set of facts. If I understand your still-to-be-born opus, you want the young to think for themselves. That is precisely what you are doing on the real stage in the play of spoken words. Defying all science, they will take away more than you are giving them. There is no greater tribute for you as a teacher, no greater act of intellectual openness and honesty."

She sighed, gazed into those attentive eyes, clasped the hand closest to her and entwined her fingers with his. "I am pleased no end that you have confided in me about these thoughts. Justin you have succeeded where so many others have failed. You should bask in the harvest."

Her words rested peacefully with him at the time as well as later when he dwelled upon them. There was no magic formula for rightness. There was merely the common sense that displayed what he should have known himself. He was trying to calm a seething spirit, to tame it for constructive development. It confirmed the need for his book to reach a wider audience. It reassured him that he might be helpful in some small way.

> *They who know the truth are not equal to those who love it, and they who love it are not equal to those who find pleasure in it* [China].

SEVENTEEN

At least one feat had been mastered, one obstacle removed. As he took his place before the class, he did not need the obvious signs to know that he could now teach and inspire, unimpeded by cross-currents. He saw it in their eyes, sensed it in the way that Ted Amherst sat so attentively. Estelle's involvement also appeared to be only academically charged. The silence was inviting, the expectancy keen. Kate had been so right. It was as much for him as it was for them. Emotional intellectualism undaunted.

"You are part of the underground, the new underground. It is a movement, as you well know, not confined to this university or even to this nation. Here, it is centered at Blantyre. In California it has spread from the schools onto the streets. Into the basic beliefs of the street people. Being a political scientist, this is a phenomenon I find totally engrossing and spiritually moving. It is a renouncement of the morals and provisions of the conformed society. An abandonment of it – physically, intellectually, emotionally, and economically. It is an attack on the established order. A sign of hostility to authority and a denial of traditional assumptions about life, literature, and politics. It is an assault on the basic principle upon which society is built – that it is more sacred to make money than to be a good person. Your spokesmen in the underground press portray it all vividly. Let me read to you some excerpts from an April 1967 article by Guy Strait in Maverick magazine:

The straight world is a jungle of taboos,
Fears, and personality games.

He calls it the *Shrine of Squaredom*, the dehumanizing of society.

The terrible truth is that our prosperity
is the bringer of misery. We have been
brainwashed by the advertising industry
with being the most dissatisfied people
in the world. We are told we must all
be handsome or beautiful, sexually
devastating, and owners of a staggering
amount of recreational gadgetry or doomed
to frustration. The result is that most
of us are frustrated.

Eban Given in the September 1, 1967 issue of <u>Avatar</u> magazine describes us as a world of sleepwalkers:

Beings completely turned off to the
underlying meaning of the trial and
drudgery of their existence. Defenseless
in the deluges of sensations that fall
on their heads like snow and bury them
under so that they can no longer stand
upright but only crawl like moles beneath
the surface of the swirling drifts holding
each other's tails in their teeth.

This is the *me-tooism* at any price – the coercive requisite of immoral philosophical similarity. Society makes individuals feel guilty so that they will not act. The degeneration of an age."

A pause to confirm that every eye was riveted on his face, every ear open to the sound of his voice. "Your movement even is developing a language of its own. You are dropping out, turning on, and tuning in. The movement is taking many different forms in various places. But with amazing similarity in philosophical overtones. The Free Speech Movement in Berkeley. In New York City, the Head Shop and the Psychedelicatessan, ushering in a new cult of love. The Black People's Free Store in the Haight-Fillmore section, which besides being a free store also communicates love to fellow human beings. Then there are the Diggers in Haight-Ashbury. The Diggers are street people who take their name from the 17th Century British communal group that took possession of land after the Civil War, tilling it in the name of the people, and giving the food away. It has no leaders, only spokesmen. The Digger *modus operandi* is DO YOUR THING. Helen Swich Perry, in her book, <u>The Human Be-In</u>, describes the hippie philosophy as *each person has his thing and is continually in the process of rediscovering it; but he is in a moving sea of humanity in which his thing becomes a significant part of the general process.* The Provos are a branch of the hippie phenomenon. The street is used as a stage and activity there is an end in itself. Game play is used to corrode the established values and order. Nothing is held on to and catharsis is resolved through the pseudo-event that makes fun and absurdity of the real one. Yes, you are all in a period of self-imposed exile. Erik Erikson calls it the *psycho-social moratorium.* Allen Ginsberg describes the responsibility of a new order that is to be the community of the heart. Richard E. Farson has espoused even a Bill of Rights:

The Right to Leisure
The Right to Health
The Right to Beauty
The Right to Truth
The Right to Intimacy
The Right to Travel
The Right to Study
The Right to Sexual Fulfillment
The Right to Altruism
The Right to Be Different

Notable are the Seven deadly Sins according to Mahatma Gandhi:

Commerce without ethics;
Knowledge without character;
Measure without conscience;
Politics without principle;
Science without humanity;
Wealth without work;
Worship without sacrifice.

Most contemporary commentators identify the Berkeley explosion of 1964 as the start of the student revolt. George Paloczi-Hovarth, in his recent book, Youth Up In Arms, however, states that in fact it was prepared by the United States Educational Policy Commission that defined the goal of American schools in 1951 as *the pursuit of happiness* and in 1961 as *the ability to think.* He states pointedly that the university student has never been fully accepted as a regular member of society, and the university is the greatest failure of our time because the universities do not offer the kind of wisdom now needed to save mankind from itself and its successes. It is not part of *respectable scholarship.* The prevalent thought among students is that the industrial-military complex corrupts universities. George F. Kennan presents the counter argument in his book Democracy and the Student Left, in which he says that the student left misconceives the function of the university. Swept up as they are with causes, injustice and social problems, they should be in a setting that is merely one uninterrupted current events course. The function of the university is to assist the young to learn about life in its wider and more permanent aspects and to tap something of the accumulated wisdom of the ages about the nature of man and his predicament."

He paused long enough to draw in a deep breath. "So, what is reality? Have all of the vital aspects of human nature been all but eliminated by the conditions of modern society? Are you basically a deviate subculture? Are your energies misdirected? Are you Rorschach radicals, as descriptively labeled by one observer? What is wisdom? What is truth? How does learning fit into the grand scheme? These are some of the hard questions that you, the American young, must face in the light of severe criticism and revulsion by your elders, as well as by the very institution whose chairs you occupy. Should that institution comport with you, or should it be compatible with what you desire to take from it? Or, in fact, is there and might there be a middle ground? Perhaps, most important of all, what does it all mean for you as an individual? Beyond that, what does it represent for you and for all of us as members of the national and world communities? Ancient Chinese philosophers believed that man could not be expected to revere that which chastised him. This is not unlike modern thought portraying that any attempt to deal with the system makes you a victim of it. But, what are the viable, long-term alternatives? A people's store? A Digger way-of-life? These are commendable actions for the short-term. They may prove to be too impractical for the long-term and on a large-scale. Too often those who defend minority rights while on campus wind up being the abuser or ignorer of those rights when part of the majority later on. I don't profess to have all the answers or solutions. As is obvious, I know more of the questions than answers, but it is a starting point. As H.L. Mencken satirically observed: *For every difficult and complex problem, there is an obvious solution that is simple, easy and wrong.* Yet, I hope that during the forthcoming weeks we will be able to explore together not only our own aspirations but also some possible alternatives, some of the kinds of personal commitments you can make to right your lives and better the world around you. A choice of actions is not easy, particularly if a desired harmony between personal direction and humanity's future is at stake. To be flexible with choices, adventuresome in experimentation, and humble in the face of failures. To be outward looking and forward thinking. No boundaries. No formalities. Etched in the marble around the walls of the Great Hall at the Library of Congress are sayings of great wisdom. One of these reads: *Too low they build who build beneath the stars.* The greater the expectation, the greater the accomplishment. A portion of an article written by Michael McClure called *Poison Wheat* in the San Francisco Oracle in 1967 reads:

> *An arena must be cleared for new thought and action*
> *that is not national in scope*

but incorporates all human creatures . . .
and all creatures to come!
All who move to the stars to investigate
The possibilities of infinite freedoms.

Words to ponder well beyond this classroom, beyond today."

The quiet in the room served as a natural break. The students turned nearly in unison towards Ted. His newfound enlightenment, yet unrevealed in the visual process, began its subtle emergence when he merely shrugged his shoulders and smiled slightly. It was interpreted as a signal by the others that he was passing on any primary opportunity and responsibility to comment on all that had been said, thereby leaving the floor open to any other protagonist.

For a fleeting moment Justin gazed upon Estelle's face, seeing in the instant the warmth and vitality sparkling in her eyes and a gentle smile appeared on the delicate mouth. He basked in her radiance.

Several hands were raised. "Since this is a seminar, you need not raise your hand to speak. Just go at it; let your spirit guide your freedom of expression. If we run out of time to hear all of the remarks, we will pick up there at the next session."

The voice of a young woman in the rear was the first to be heard. A silky voice, with perfect and cultured diction. He studied the determined face, forever putting away the thought that the young are unprovocative, unexciting, and sheepish. "I have listened to all you have said, as we all have, and it is obvious that you are trying to stimulate our thinking. Perhaps, it is all a question of outlook, or outreach. But, I think we ought to dwell upon the concept of experimentation that you raised. Aren't each of us, and all of us, including the university and our elders, in a stage or series of experiments? Trial and error so-to-speak. We look at it as trying to improve things, while the staid generations merely look for our errors so that they can make a public spectacle of our going wrong or being unworthy to have our own ideas. They make a mockery of our failures. Then, we are all consumed in trying to defend ourselves rather than trying a new avenue of approach, looking for fresh concepts. They make a mockery of our existence."

"Yes," Justin responded slowly and deliberately, "We are constantly in stages of experimentation. Young people can get away with much that they do. The important point to remember is that the experimenting is not just for the now but new ideas and projecting alternative life styles should consider long-range goals. The effects of today's actions may not emerge immediately. Margaret Meade in her book Culture and Commitment indicates that the young, unburdened by historical conditioning, now set the tone and raise the issues society has to deal with. Also, in another interesting book, Henry Malcolm in Generation of Narcissus portrays an unusual and perhaps very enlightened observation of the generation gap. He feels that parents in spite of what they may think actually have succeeded with their children by liberating them. They have reared them to be self-motivated, expressive, and autonomous, and that is just what you all are. Where parents have failed is in their own society because they have left the world intact, a world that demands different attitudes than those they have instilled in their progeny. Society belongs only to the establishment. The liberalism of your parents is not the liberalism you are experimenting with. Therefore, the young are forced to take all of the risks and pay the personal price that an uncharted future presents. If you are ridiculed for mistakes, take that as a sign of strength rather than weakness. Perhaps they are afraid that when all is said and done you will have succeeded where they have failed."

The bell rang, nearly as an appropriate response to the end of his thought conveyance. The students gathered up their books and left reluctantly, almost as if they were about to approach something meaningful and the system found yet another way to deny them the full benefits of it. Even time can be an oppressor. Justin knew better.

Who waits for time, loses time [Italy].

Time was everyone's enemy. He lingered in the empty room, a thoughtful contrast to the fullness that he felt in his mind and heart.

EIGHTEEN

Estelle delayed her rush to the next class, lingering in the hall hoping that Justin would catch up with her for a brief exchange. It was with some surprise that she glanced at the man besides her. Ted looked deeply into her eyes. "I was hoping to get you alone for a moment. There is much I have to tell you, more than I can probably adequately explain."

Momentarily stunned at hearing his unexpected voice as well as the shock of hearing any expression from him that might indicate a human frailty, she set up an appropriate guard, "I will be late for my next class."

"I just wanted to tell you that I have changed. I am different. If I were a religious person, I would even go so far as to say I have been saved. Ironically, I may have been saved in a way. I have seen the light, a kind of illumination anyway. I am abandoning my participation in this student business, and concentrating on my own future. That sounds selfish, I know."

She asked herself, "Is this really Ted Amherst?" Outwardly, she tried not to express too much of an interest, still harboring a sense of hurt and disappointment concerning their prior relationship. "Well, I am happy for you, if you feel you are doing what is right. But, what, if I may ask, has brought on such a metamorphosis?"

"Candidly, it is the by-product of a Dr. Post inspiration. I think I never had a sensible idol. All of my true images existed either in literature or in my head. But, I would be a fool if I did not recognize things as they are." He took a deep breath and said earnestly, "My one true regret is that I did not recognize that you had also represented that same kind of challenge, a similar opportunity for me to look at me. I am truly sorry we did not ….. and could not ….. have had more."

She could not help but melt a bit under this strange confession. It was eye opening to learn that he was, after all, a sensitive person. Perhaps, it justified in some small way the time she had thought she had wasted with him. That potential must have been there, and in some mysterious way she must have recognized it. Especially was she gladdened by the tribute by Ted of Justin's accomplishment in reaching him and turning him around. That just served to reinforce even more the deep love she felt for this miracle man who had come so forcefully into their lives and was having such a dramatic impact on them. "Ted, I must be going, but I do appreciate you telling me this. Our time has passed, but strangely I feel closer to you at this moment than I did throughout our physical relationship. This may be the essence of the brotherhood-sisterhood we all seek in our peers. I wish you every happiness. Some time you can fill me in on the details of your personal discovery. I would really like to know how and why this transformation came about. I, too, have found some unanticipated answers and have gone through a major upheaval. I have grown up. Maybe that is an oversimplification, but I am also very different from what I was. There is a new me, the real me."

"No grudge then," he said almost like a little boy after a fistfight.

She smiled broadly, sending a heartthrob through his system. "I hold no grudges. Life is too beautiful for that kind of unconstructive distraction."

As she turned to go off, he said after her in a whisper that she could not hear. "We were good for each other after all."

As Justin stepped into the hallway, he caught a glimpse of Estelle moving away from Ted's side. It was obvious that the two of them had been talking. He was sure that he would hear about it later. As he approached Ted, he discovered that the young man was off in the distance deep in thought. A blank expression filled his face. "I see my talk put you to sleep standing on your feet."

Ted turned to him with surprise. "To the contrary. I think I finally achieved the ultimate success with you coming around to see our point-of-view. The others probably feel I am writing your material, and I probably wouldn't deny it. But, you and I know that you are an original. You probably won't believe this, but I admire that in a person."

"One does not need material to convey the sentiments of our times. We all should feel them. I sense that in spite of all outward appearances you and I are not as divergent as one might think."

"Yes. There is a great deal of truth in that. I have been going through a period of introspection and have made some important personal decisions about myself. You might say I was overdue for change."

Justin smiled. He could not help but like this earnest youth, both for his challenges and his expressive ability. He would probably never know that he was instrumental in bringing all of this out in him. "Any thinking, feeling person is ready for change. That is the genuine harvest. The true nourishment of our being."

"Well, I suppose the bottom line is that I am no longer your adversary. In fact, I may very well become your strongest ally. I am giving up the cause celebre."

"I am a bit surprised. You seem like a natural leader, and it is necessary to have leaders. Leaders who know who they are and where they are taking their cause are important elements in creative progress with minimal hurt."

Ted looked off in the direction that Estelle had gone. "I owe something to myself first, I suppose. I was postponing that through the medium of involvement, but I now have a more urgent need. My personal challenge has leaped to the forefront of my life, and it is consuming all of my waking energies. It is what I must give top priority to."

Justin thought to himself that the wild horse's head had been turned. "Self-discovery can be a powerful antidote as well as being a most satisfying exploration. Isn't it?"

"Yes. And, I would like to talk about it with you some day."

"I would like that too. Any time. The chasm has been closed between us, I am sure, and a friendship has been born."

"I would like to be your friend. It will take some time before I sort out my prospects before we can talk at length. But, I definitely would want to do that. I never thought that I could befriend an older generation type, but as you say, there is no gulf between us now. You are more like me than per-haps I am like you." With that he turned rigidly, and walked off with a slow yet confident gait. The world was there for his conquest, and he had to pre-pare for it. He left Justin feeling older than his own years implied.

Through the doorway to his office, at first he only noticed the long hair and the small framed back, and when she heard him enter and turned towards him, he noticed that she was too young to be one of his students.

"Dr. Post?" Her voice was shaky and hesitant.

"Yes," he said carefully as he moved around to sit at the desk.

"I am Rita Mington. This note will tell you why I am here." From the pocket of her denim jacket she took out a small folded piece of paper and handed it to him.

> *Buttercup,*
>
> *Even with this note, I take the coward's way out. By the time you read it I will be gone to another city, another opportunity to become worthy of you as well as myself. I will be out of all your lives , where I must be. I am truly sorry for all of the hurt I have caused, particularly with you and Suzie. I have left you all rea-sonably secure financially, but if you need anything else see Dr. Post at the University, a teacher that I have recently had confi-dence in. In my own way I love you, and I always will. Please forgive me.*
>
> > *DAD*

After reading the words and noticing the lack of hand control over the writing, he tried to be expressionless as he handed it back to her. "Sit down, Rita, please."

She sat slowly, timidly, in the small chair before the desk.

It was several minutes before either spoke, both appraising the other in their own circumspection. For Rita, it had taken a great deal of courage to come to see a perfect stranger. But, she had no one else to turn to. Her moth-er had immersed herself in her own personal detailed life enterprises, and her sister was staying at the school more often with less and less reason to return home. Where did that leave her? Who would explain to her what was happening, and what would become of her? She felt a burning need to try and understand what made adults so complex, so void of feeling. Was her own sensitivity and concern abnormal? Why should she feel pain because her father, a man she barely knew anymore, had left? Should she just accept what life has to offer, including all of its sadness and depression, without questioning it and with no effort exerted to change it or overcome it?

For Justin, as he stared into the young face, he saw Dr. Mington's eyes, and he felt a great compassion swell within his breast. He saw the pretty features, the fresh complexion, and the dainty hands with fingers slightly trembling, and he sensed that here was another troubled individual whose path was to cross with his. It was all becoming a blur. Lives, miseries, and his own personal dilemma and desires. It might not even accomplish anything to try and sort it all out. The one image that was starting to come closer into focus was that it is painful to be human, and that a helping hand and a kind word are needed by so many. There appears to be one element so vital for inner strength. The knowing that there is someone close by who cares, one who really wants to know and to be of help.

As hard as she tried, and as gallantly as she had sworn to herself that she would not do it, she felt her lower lip quiver and the tears came rapidly to fill her eyes. For the hundredth time she had tried to grapple with the larger picture, the significance of it all, but the only thing that seemed real was the hurt that she felt. The sorrow and despair not only for herself but also for her mother and sister. She had been the closest to her father at one time, a long time ago, and that is probably what hurt the most. Now, she had to know, to understand why he had run away. "I really don't know what I am doing here. But, I feel like I have no other place to turn to. I need to know why he left." The tears flowed unabated, and the sobbing racked her entire body.

Doubting that she knew what had actually transpired between her father and Estelle, and quickly calculating that it would be best if all that was left untold, he grasped at some comforting words to assist this troubled young lady in righting her world. "I really don't know. I am new here at the University, and I did not get a chance to know him all that well. But, something was bothering him, that I am sure of, and I had a good impression that he just did not know how to handle it. Maybe it was a professional failure. People in high positions for long periods of time lose sight of the day-to-day small accomplishments and they lose their perspective. They get to a point where without a major accomplishment they feel that they are either doing nothing or whatever they do it is not being done well."

She responded starting in a slow, soft manner, that increased in tone and pace as she proceeded. "I know he hadn't written anything for a long time. His last book was about ten years ago, and it was not favorably reviewed. But, he has been so totally withdrawn. He has been acting strangely for a long time. There was no emotion on his part, no display of feeling for me, nothing for my mother. It was like a dagger in her heart, I know, although she would never talk about it. She has been like an empty shell, and I feel such pity for her. It is hell for me living in that kind of situation. I tried not to let it get me down, but it does. It seems to be getting worse. There is no answer, I guess, for why it is or why it has to be that way. If I can't escape from my own thoughts, where do I go?"

Justin, taking a deep breath, calmly explained what he felt should be said. "There are some things we never can know, or even if we knew them we might not be able to understand them. Something evidently drove him away. Something drove him into the way that he was, and something happened or didn't happen that he was probably counting on. I seriously doubt that it had anything to do with you, or even your mother. It was something that he would not or could not face, and I think he made a decision that he felt was best for all of you. I also think he would like to see you carry on in the most sensible way possible. That means concentrating on yourself, preparing yourself for growing up to be as mature and responsible as possible. You must accept that all of this is his problem and not yours. I cannot give you answers. But I think he sent you to see me because he knew that I would want to help if I can, and to, most of all, be your friend. We may not reach any conclusions, but I am willing to talk it out with you whenever it all gets bottled up."

She gazed intently on his warm smile, and she felt more relaxed and even relieved. Somehow, that was the kind of answer and reassuring voice that she would have expected from her father, her real father if he had remained as she had remembered him when she was a child. Here it was coming from a stranger. It would not surprise her if her father had taken over this stranger's body. Maybe he had submitted himself to an experiment with the Science Department, and as part of it all he had been transformed into a new being, and just did not know how to tell her about it. If it had been going on for years, that might easily explain all the events leading up to this end. Her father, however, could not be able to hide all of the telltale signs from her. She smiled back, cunningly.

"It is good to see you smile. You're a lovely girl, and a smile is the paramount beauty. It is the most personal of attributes. You have a great secret weapon there. Enough to devastate any mortal soul."

The question quickly formed in her mind, "What did he mean by that?" The whole happening was turning into a mystery all right, the kind of intrigue that she might very well find irresistible. Or, was he flirting with her? He was cute. But, she would not know what to make of that. Her experience with boys was quite limited, and she had never been attracted to or by an older man before. Yet, she could not deny that any new experience at this point might be just what she needed to spring her from this depressing cloud that hung over her.

For him, he was sorry he had said what he did, for he was perceptive enough to notice that it was not received as intended. Wanting to lighten the air, to be even witty, he had ventured those casual remarks anticipating that they might help her feel better about herself. After she left, he regretted the utterance even more. Undoubtedly, here was another female complication in his life. Rita was evidently seeking a father figure, more than perhaps an explanation of what had happened. That certainly was nothing he had any kind of preparation for, and was ill equipped to handle. He had a premonition that there would be few choices available to him. It was another situation thrust upon him, and he would have to make the best of it. While longing for a basic simplicity, his immersion in complexity was baffling. Yet, there was something very promising about it all. If, somehow, he could straighten it all out, handle it adequately, then perhaps he could well emerge from all past guilt and face a brighter, more rewarding personal future. If nothing else, his present involvement did prevent him from being haunted by his past as much as before. Or, was his past actually his present? Or, the present his past? Of little difference to be sure. Whatever it was or is, he had to confront it.

NINETEEN

The Thanksgiving break did not represent a problem. Both Kate and Estelle had invited Justin to go home with them for the holiday to meet their families, but he was successful in persuading them both that Christmas might be a more opportune time. Postponement as a temporary reprieve. He would meet that inevitable conflict soon enough. A strict adherence to that enterprising philosophy of not worrying about ominous events until they are actually upon us. In the mean time, anything could happen which might change the apparent drift of events.

So, as he had hoped, he would be alone during that brief period of time. Time and effort devoted to him. A precious luxury. To sort out and take stock of his being. Yet, when Rita invited him over for Thanksgiving dinner, he could tell by the intensity of her voice that it was important to her. They had had numerous lengthy and detailed discussions since their initial conversation. He had found her to be an extremely bright and discerning young woman, revealing much of her father's scholarly interests and aptitude. Occasionally, he even noticed a playful sparkle in her eyes, and he could not help but be taken with the freshness and youthful vitality that this new found friendship filled him with.

While it might be awkward to be there at the Mington home, in the presence of her mother and sister, he felt that in some small way he might make this a slightly better time for them. Holidays were probably an especially difficult period for them. Since he had lost his own family, he knew what the sensation was like. Not that he could ever be a replacement, but merely the supplier of a momentary diversion.

Arriving at the Mington home about mid-afternoon, he was greeted by Rita at the door. She had put her dark hair up in a bun and she looked older than her real tender years. Mrs. Mington had been drinking, and all of the obvious signs were there. Her eyes rolled, and her speech was disjointed and slurred. Rita had told him that she had been drinking more and more lately, and that she would often drink herself into a state of obliviousness. An easy escape route from the disappointments and hurts. Yet, an escape only to face a new and angrier evil. The noticeable dragging effect on those who are closeby and who witness the act of self-destruction. A very sad state of affairs to watch unfold, pathetic to those who have to live through it and with it. For a child to watch it all unfurl is particularly cruel. Young lives should not have to witness that sort of human deterioration. They cannot handle the mixture of guilt and shame.

Fortunately, Suzie was not there. She had been invited to a boy friend's home in Boston for the holiday. While she had felt badly leaving Rita to bear the burden alone, for her there was no choice to ponder over. Rita did not blame her, and had even encouraged her to take advantage of the opportunity to partake of some sane moments with a real family.

Midway through the dinner, Mrs. Mington silently slipped off. Rita helped her into bed. Then they finished the meal in silence, and it was not until they had cleaned off the table and were in the kitchen that they spoke at all. She washed the dishes, and he stood close by her side and dried them.

"I'm sorry, Justin. I meant this to be a pleasant, warm time for you. I should have known better, but I did not want you to spend the holiday by yourself. I am sure that you feel awkward, and I hope that you forgive me."

"Rita, there is nothing to forgive you for. Your intentions and efforts were wonderful. The food was great, and being in your company watching you handle such a difficult situation with grace and maturity is uplifting. For a person who does not have a family of his own, you are my family."

"I might just as well not have a family either. I am not sure I ever did. The last thing I wanted today was to be alone. My thoughts are very poor company. Mom is getting worse every day, and I just don't know what to do about it. I can't handle this alone."

"There are organizations equipped to help people in just these kinds of situations. It can be a benefit and very comforting just to talk with others who are going through similar experiences."

"Yes. I know about them. I may do that at some future time. Right now I feel I must try to keep this as private as possible. No one knows, besides you, exactly what is happening. Even Suzie does not know the full story. I have so far been able to keep it behind these walls. The organizations she works with, as well as her friends, would be shocked if they knew. And, if she knew that they knew, she would never step out of this house again or worse. She is like a child. I suppose I keep hoping for a miracle. Like he will just walk through the door and we can turn the clock back ...... way back ...... and start over fresh. Useless dreams, I know. Funny, how for a young person I feel so utterly old. I don't laugh the way I used to. I have little interest in anything except the books that I can bury myself in. My attention is easily swayed from the so-called normal things. I have no interest in school or school related activities. Even my friends, none of whom were ever really close ones, have gotten the message and do not attempt to talk to me or even contact me any more. I guess I am pretty envious of those who can pick and choose what happens to them in life. For me, it seems to be all thrust upon me. No choices, no options. Just bleak and very depressing tomorrows."

"Rita, I truly understand how difficult it is for you to be trapped in an adult role long before you should have to be. It short-changes the frivolity and spontaneity of your young years. But, I have been so impressed by your maturity, your ability to handle yourself and to fully perceive the significance of the situations you are involved in. Most young people cannot see things that clearly. Your experience appears ageless. You are not old in the sense that you feel that way but old to the point of knowing and having the ability that goes with it. That should make you feel very good about yourself. It has to build the necessary confidence for you to participate in an adult world and to make the necessary decisions that such a life demands. Very few people get to pick the path they will travel on through life. In the last analysis, I dare say it is not the choices that are important but the way we manage the places along that road that we find ourselves travelling on. From all that I have observed, you are a master traveler."

She could not say the words, or even remember them with precision. However, the connotation languished in her mind as if she were reading them again. The feeling of being comfortable with a person, of being safe with a person you do not have to weigh your thoughts or measure your words with. The person with the faithful hand that will take them and sift through them, and with a breath of kindness blow the rest away.

She wiped her hands on the apron and removed it slowly. "Come into the living room. I'll pour some wine."

Side by side they sat on the sofa. He swirled the wine in its glass, the deep red color briefly reflecting thoughts untold. She gently took the glass from him and sipped some of its contents. "That, Justin, is to symbolize that we drink from the same cup of life. Your company and support are very valuable to me. I don't feel so totally alone when you are near. I .... I love you, you know."

He reached for her delicate hand. "Love is a very strong word. You love me in the sense that I am willing to help you overcome difficult times, to stand by you. It is the love for a brother."

"Perhaps. But, love is love. As the saying goes, *I have to say what I feel, and feel what I say.*"

"There are various kinds of love. I have grown to love you as well, a love nurtured by the qualities of wholesomeness and purity that you exude. A freshness and intelligence that leads a child's innocence to cope with a cruel adult world. The admiration that comes from watching one so ably do what has to be done."

"I cannot cope alone. I would not want to."

As a momentary silence prevailed, even though she could not remember the poet's name, again she could not help but recall some other words she had recently melded into her storehouse of beautiful thoughts, to be released at warm, inviting periods such as this.

In the chilly hours and minutes of uncertainty – I want to be –
in the warm hold of your lovin' mind
To feel you all around me and to take your hand – along the sand –

Ah but I may as well try and catch the wind.
When sundown pales the sky I want to hide awhile – behind your smile
  – and everywhere I look your eyes I'd find
For me to love you now would be the sweetest thing – 'twould make
  me sing
Ah but I may as well try and catch the wind.
When rain has hung the leaves with tears – I want you near – to kill
  my fears
to help me to leave all my blues behind
For standing in your heart is where I want to be – and long to be –
Ah but I may as well try and catch the wind.

She put on the radio, adjusting the stations until a slow foxtrot played. "Will you dance with me, kind sir?"

He took her in his arms, and she pressed her head to his shoulder. The sweet fragrance of her hair filled his nostrils. Slowly, she looked up at him, and he kissed her lightly. The small lips sweetly joined his. He felt her budding breasts as she pressed tightly against him. "Justin, please love me."

"I do love you, in a very special way." He was sensitive to her need for some expression of love, of caring, to ease her plight. A demonstrative sign to reassure her that he would continue to care, continue to be there for whatever encouragement he might bring to her troubled mind.

"Please, Justin, make love to me. I want you."

Hugging her even closer, Justin sighed. "Rita. Rita. You must understand. Not all love is physical, nor can it always be. I do love you, and in a way that is very dear to me. You occupy a very special place in my heart. It has a great deal of meaning for me. I will always want you to be a part of my life. The beauty of our being close is in the purity of our sharing problems and beginnings. But, it cannot and should not be as a physical love commitment between a man and a woman. There can be closeness, there can be sensitivity, and there can be a joining without the bodily consummation. Believe me, that is also love. It can be one of the most enduring of loves."

He did not have to see the tears. The voice was choked up, the body heaving gently with the sobbing. "But, I need that assurance of your love.

How can I feel it without our bodies joining? I do not need a brother. I need a partner."

"The real worth, and the lasting benefit, is in the believing and the knowing that it is there. The reservoir that you can draw from to quench all of your thirsts and dire needs. It is the energy that you can tap when you need just that extra bit more to overcome a troubling experience. While sex can be a manifestation of love, the root of it all is in that knowing, in that powerful feeling. If our hearts join as I embrace you like this, isn't that satisfying?"

Holding her slim body against him, his compassion stretched to its outer limits. It seemed like one emotional involvement after another. How much could he spread himself out before it took its toll on him? Yet, how could he possibly even consider turning his back to any one of the testing additions to his life? They represented as much for him as he did for them. Perhaps he had taken too much from life already. These opportunities to give of himself seemed almost to be preset, prearranged. The message becoming clearer was that such might be his role in life. For making one woman so unhappy in the past, atonement was taking the form of leading other numerous women to a more promising future. Or, was he just kidding himself? Was it the same old selfish mannerism taking hold in what may be the most devilish form of all?

Rita's head was swirling. She had never been possessive, but her life had been changed so drastically. Recent events had brought her current position so clear to her. She had no one. For all purposes, her father had deserted her years ago. Her mother was now useless, and could not be counted on for anything. Her sister was gradually growing distant from her, becoming a stranger. Now, this kindly man represented stability and a security that she sensed could help her to survive and be productive. She yearned for his soothing voice, his gentle touch. Her reeling and romantic mind projected a role for her of mutual fulfillment. Her mind and body were just beginning to blossom. Her inspiration to flower could no longer come from just the books and poetry that she loved. It was to be from this man, of that she was now sure. She had to be strong enough and smart enough to satisfy him. To prove to him that he also needed her to the exclusion of all other women. To accomplish that feat, she had to be able to do more for him than any other woman might do. More than any other woman would ever do. Her young years could be an asset, a stimulant. She returned his embrace with a cunning submissiveness. This new found power of love would help her prevail. Heaven help any one or any thing that stood in her way.

TWENTY

Spending the vacation time at home did not turn out to be an enjoyable time for Estelle. She had missed Justin and longed deeply for his companionship. While making her feel good about herself in that it reinforced the strong feelings that she had, the pang of temporary emptiness was burdensome. She pined for his physical comforting, as well as for the mental well being his force represented. Worse of all was the widening gap with her parents because of this. When she told them about Justin, they were not nearly as understanding as she had expected. In fact, they were nearly hostile. It really amazed her how for all of her life she had sensed, or at least thought in her own mind that she truly had, the understanding and full support of her parents. Faced with the seriousness of her expressions about this newly found love, all of the trite cliches came out. They presented such an ugly image of what he could represent to her young and fruitful life, all without meeting or wanting to give him a chance to present to them what so readily appeared to her. She found herself cringing at their words and regretting their company. Even if they had been non-committal, aloof, patient to see what direction it might take, she would have accepted such a stance graciously. She might have even respected that kind of open and sincere position. As it was, however, the only thing that they succeeded in doing was to drive that proverbial wedge between parent and child, and in doing so only compelled a stronger willingness on her part for further involvement in the relationship. A pronounced overreaction that has damaged all of those years of closeness. While not irrevocable, she knew that her feelings and communication with them would now have to be guarded. A protective blanket can smother just as easily as it can be beneficial.

Back on campus, she sensed something was wrong. The first thing that she did was to call him, and she was hurt that her immediate desire to see him was not reciprocated. After all, he could not really have been that busy since he had gone nowhere over the holiday.

The mood on campus was different as well. There was much more open talk of direct action against the university authorities. Stories were spreading of possible takeovers of buildings, as had been done earlier on other campuses. Confrontations with officials and law enforcement personnel were anticipated. The students were noticeably restless, more vocal, and openly antagonistic. She shuddered, realizing that things were precariously unsettling. She felt all too strongly that it might all get worse, much worse. Too many influences, too many possible circumstances for her to have total control over her surroundings and the direction of her life. Her destiny was evidently slipping from her grasp. A chill seeped into the deepest recesses of her body. Her body trembled under its influence. Even full attention on her intellect could not shake off this foreboding premonition.

The thought crossed her mind of talking to Ted, to take advantage of their newly acquainted compatibility. But, she could not help but feel that this aspect of her life was behind her and that she would be better off leaving that part undisturbed. It might even prove to be a step backwards. Involvement might be culminated, but sublimated regrets would tinge any real closeness. Out of pure selfishness she did not want any other facet of her life to intrude on what she had found with Justin. To bask in the discovered love was the only sure cozy place in this cold world for her, and she so desperately wanted to affix herself to that magical glow. Any infringement would most definitely be unwelcome.

When was she going to see him? The sense of uneasiness was heightened considerably. The telephone impression was upsettingly correct. When they did meet, his embrace was tentative. The postponement of lovemaking was left unexplained.

Stating the obvious gave her no comfort. "Justin. Something is wrong, isn't it?"

Justin's position lacked a foundation. He did love her, even if he could not fully explain to himself why. It would be far better to reassure her than to meet head on with a decision that he was not prepared to make or to justify. "No, not really. I just have so much on my mind. I am discovering nerves I never thought I had. I had even half expected to start on my book over the break, but each attempt to start it met with internal resistance. I look back on the time when writing came so easily to me. I realize that as a sideline observer, it is so much easier not to be judgmental and to be unemotional. Being a player, and the whole picture changes. The nature of the beast is devouring me, not the other fellow."

"Are you sure that is all there is to it? I don't mean to make light of your turmoil. It is just that I love you so much. I can't bear not sharing everything you feel, even the frustrations and uncertainties."

He embraced her tightly. "I love you for that sense of wholeness. Yet, it all seems to be pressing down on me with an unbearable weight. There is nothing that can be done except for me to sort it all out in my head. It's all my problem, I assure you. The understanding person that you are, and my emotional tie to you is undisturbed and impenetrable."

However, in his own mind the problem was crystallizing. The nagging doubt that he had about handling these several involvements was sharpening the real issue. Was he being fair to them? Did they have to know it all to decide whether or not to accept him on his own terms? Or, was it enough that they were deriving satisfaction from the existing relationships as they seemed to be? His lack of honesty with himself extended out to them, and the results might be hurtful. Did he have any right to impose such harm on others? It was contrary to his philosophy and conflicted with what he hoped was the goodness of his being. Strange, ever so strange, he had been able to develop a subject expertise over the years and in his field of endeavor he was a master of creativity and diversity. He could predict results with near precision. Yet, with relationships with the opposite sex, ever since his debacle with Rosalind, he had been groping in the dark. A weak mind and an even weaker will governed his actions. He did not know in the slightest where it was all taking him and what might happen next. This sharp discrepancy bothered him the most. Why should human emotions be any different than political science in the nature of theory and practice? The heart is the culprit.

Measure thy cloth ten times, thou canst cut it but once [Russia].
You don't have to cut down the tree to get at the fruit [Cambodia].

They discussed the unfolding events at the University at length. She voiced concern for his personal safety, but he dismissed that as being unlikely. Such was the least of his worries. Yet, both were aware of how situations can get out of hand. The shooting by the National Guard of students at Kent State in 1970 was shocking news to verify such possibilities. More and more stories involving violence as a means of expression, as a commanding way of obtaining results. All attesting to the growing unsettling atmosphere that pervaded these academic halls. Peaceful and loving ways quickly become vestiges of the past. Another evil attributable to impatience.

The prospects were bleak for compromise and settlement. Disruptions were a definite possibility, and the field was open beyond that depending on perceptions or misperceptions. A nation at war with itself, only on a smaller scale. A morbid but significant comparison. Total energy in the war effort demanding great risks and sacrifices. Individual gratification and personal aspirations pushed aside, shoved into the background.

"Justin," she said suddenly, "I am scared, very scared for all of us. Strange how I used to think that the unknown was exciting. Perhaps, it was because I always felt that whatever it turned out to be I would make it to the other side. Now, I don't have that same optimistic outlook. That's why I think these moments .... here and now ...... have such great meaning for me. Is it possible that this is all that there is? That this is all there will ever be?"

"Perhaps that has been the great sociological malady of recent generations. The entire, or at least seemingly total preoccupation with the future. I am becoming more of a firm believer in the here and now. It is the present that really counts. When I think back on all of my years of schooling, the consuming dedication to write and get myself established as a future scholar, there seems little meaning now for all of that action. It was wasted time and energy. I could easily dwell on what I missed because of that absorption, what I could have done instead. Rather than all that preparation for the so-called future, I could have been living and experimenting. When all is said and done, I am not sure if those things I did prepared me for anything that is logically or realistically connected with the art of living. For you and me, as well as for all of us, this is the moment to capture."

"What about the whole notion of having something to look forward to, to plan for?"

"Look forward to in the sense that if it doesn't happen then there is monumental disappointment or, at the very least, a sagging ego. Where does looking forward end and realistic expectations begin?"

"You know what I mean."

"Yes. I am only being my usual difficult self. You should already know me in the sense that I don't always say what I really believe. The teacher in me mixes with the activist. We cannot live as if there is no tomorrow. In most instances, we cannot detach a given present moment from its possible future consequences. As with all things, it is a matter of emphasis."

"Alright, I'll give you that. But, my young philosopher, there are some present conditions which mean nothing unless they have a future. Who can be so perceptive as to recognize that a present attention or concern might carry enormous benefits or misery later on? There is danger no matter how we act."

"Once again you have spotted the weakness in my reasoning. There is much to say for a pre-planned life, a charted course that marks the swells and calm seas. To follow a well designed script."

"I suppose. But, I still think you are beating around the bush. Now that you have spoken in generalities, how about getting down to particulars. Specifically, you and me."

He laughed loudly, a bit too loudly. "So, that is what you have been getting at."

"Yes. The last thing that I want, and the last thing that I want to give you is any extra pressure .... but to keep me going, I must know about us. I love you very much. That love makes demands on me, some of which I cannot help but pass on to you. I am, after all, an emotional weakling."

"Who isn't?"

"You."

"Perhaps, you don't know me as well as you think."

"My emotions are feelings, not thoughts. But, you are still evading the issue."

"I am not evading it. I just don't know what you want me to say."

"I don't want you to say anything, if you have nothing to say on your own. I don't want to hear anything you don't want to say."

He hugged her closely. Being with her like this was important to him, and he wanted her to know that as well as the difficulties he was confronting. "We have to wait. There are far too many unknowns, too many commitments pulling me in various directions. Know that I do love you. I say that because I mean it. At this time I cannot look beyond that. I hope you can accept that, and that it gives you a hint of promise and hope. Right now there are no clear pictures. There are too many loose ends here with my tasks. The dust has to settle before we can see the road ahead."

She could not deny that it hurt, and a little anger raised an uninvited glow to her cheeks. "I am disappointed. How can I not be? I look on our love as a thing of beauty, worth perpetuating. It can never be any good if it is one-sided, if only one sees a future for it. At the risk of being forward and demanding, traits I have never shown before, but I have also never felt anything this strongly, never been so sure of my direction, I must ask you something. Why can't we carve out a little niche for ourselves, for our future selves as well as our present selves no matter what the turn of events may be? That is consistent with everything we believe in and are struggling for. More importantly, why can't we dictate to a large degree the priority for tomorrow as well as today?"

"If only everything were that simple."

"It can be. For us, anyway."

"Well, if you are right, we will know it soon enough."

"I know it now. I feel it now."

"It is that now feeling that should be most important. I feel that same sense for now, but it endangers that feeling of well being to subject it to a future, as yet filled with undetermined risks. All I am trying to say is let's take it one step at a time. Let's reap the harvest now, and not worry about the next one just yet."

"That is easier said than done for you. How do I not worry about the most important thing in my life?"

He could do no more than to hold her even tighter. Each expression of his sought-after honesty would be matched by a new question. It was right of her to question him, for after a fashion he was also questioning himself. If there were no answers that satisfied either one of them, then the relationship was doomed. His only point was to try to make it apparent that some of the answers could not be known as yet, and a slow nurturing might even make the need for answers unnecessary. He could appreciate her position, but he also knew that time would be of benefit for her as well. Her youth was still testing her resolve. Reactions to the peer group and to the experience with Dr. Mington may not have taken final form as yet.

As for him, there was the brooding uncertainty of his past commingled with his behavioral present. Not sure where he had been, where he was going, there was little reason for him to be surprised at his own lack of direction and commitment. He was not sure what his mission was any more. If it was to find love, he had come upon more than any being could want. If he was to find or know himself, he was no longer sure how realistic a task that was. He might try to mark his existence on a scale of accomplishments, but the finite elements of his personality and desires would still be an enigma. This was certainly not the way to build up one's self-confidence. He was unsure of himself, so it was natural that he would be unsure of other things. He was floundering, and it might be sheer luck that he could stumble on the true meaning of what he was doing and what was happening to him. In a most frightening way, it was a similar scenario when he had been with Rosalind. Would the outcome parallel that experience? Would it end in a lost opportunity to have her on his terms? If a second chance ever developed, would it have to be the way that she wanted it? Her rules and her conditions. Her strong hand leading the way. Perhaps that is what he needed anyway. The realization of a second chance. Does such a thing actually exist? If it does, is it earned, willed, or merely luck? A second chance may merely be second-guessing. In any second, the second could be gone, as was the first.

TWENTY-ONE

All of Justin's previous attempts to meet with Willis Cohen had been unsuccessful. With all of the classes cancelled, it seemed as if both men now had more than enough time to meet and have the discourse both had eagerly anticipated.

Willis Cohen had been one of the more activist-oriented students in the 60's, and was a familiar entry in Justin's earlier treatise. He had been popularly nicknamed *Frilless Willis* because of his overt disdain for anything that was not common or ordinary. If it was overvalued or unique, an item immediately became suspect and subject to ridicule. He was now teaching at Blantyre in the History Department. His recently published book, *The Common Man's Approach to American History*, was as much of a no-frills approach to the subject as the man himself. He had never abandoned his radical ideas, but they, presumably, had mellowed with the aging process. He had read Justin's book several times. The two men had never met before but equal admiration was present.

The personification of the so-called *extreme element* was nothing like Justin had imagined. His small frame that supported a disproportionately oversized head seemed barely able to carry its burden. The sunken eyes appeared inadequately equipped to notice anything but the obvious. Once again emphatically underscoring the lingering mystery – what is one supposed to look like? The ideas a person has do not fashion the form and features. A person melds the conceptions in the form and substance most compatible to the will and style of the being.

The voice of this giant of his times was deceptively meek for the tempest it had aroused so often.   It was not the orator's voice that had brought quiet gatherings to major upheavals.   Yet, a leader has other qualities, and a leader that has purpose and ideals to become a symbol of an age or a movement as such overwhelms the human apparatus and overshadows the physical weaknesses.   As was to be unfolded, it was not how he said the words but what he said that proved to be influential.   Justin knew that this meeting was going to be a learning experience for him.   To reinforce his still humble outlook that he had much to learn as a novice scholar.

One of the true mysteries of any age is what makes a great mind.   Short of genius, probably the major component is the knack of capturing the spirit of the moment with intellectual fervor.   The capability of turning a thought into an emotion.   Some may say that it is the opportunist quality, but the connotation of that term is that some personal gain is involved.   Justin would rather believe that it is the common cause for shared worth and values.   That alone has a radical overtone.   Yet, upon close analysis, it is only that kind of power that does not corrupt.   Those worthy ideals are the strong building blocks for mankind.

"I like a man who is deep in thought without conversation," Willis said with polite vexation.

Wisdom consists of ten parts – nine parts of silence and one part with few words [Arabia].

"I see no need for asking questions.   Without ever meeting we know each other well.   Kindred spirits, I dare say.   Our books are our personalities written on our sleeves.   I read your first book, *Troubling Thoughts for Turbulent Times*, more than once so that I could grasp much of what you believe."

"Ah.   Spare me from the true believer!   Just give me one damn gooddoer!"   Willis then continued on a more placid level, "And, I have read your book more than once.   I would classify you as a *not quite complete critical intellectual*.   Fair enough?   And, my friend, if you had to affix a label on me, what would it read?"

"A *Left Leftist*."

"Touché. But, since men conceive, labels deceive. Personally, I think I am unclassifiable. My ideas have always been in a state of flux, perhaps more so today than ever before. A state of flux that owes no sovereign allegiance. A controversy of heresy. I am, after all, a man without a mind country. Why do we think in such limiting terms such as country anyway? It is the human world at large which holds us bondage and at the same time which sets us free. It is to that larger or largest body politic that we owe our allegiance and to which we are ultimately accountable."

Justin was already deeply immersed in the imagery of world. Here was a man bridging the static events of history, transcending time itself. Proof that there is a certain perpetuation in the human scheme of things. A mover as contrasted with a movee.

Willis continued without further encouragement. "Naturally, you want to know why I am a teacher now, and why I am at Blantyre?"

"Indeed and in fact."

"First, a college campus, especially this one with its attraction for old and young radicals, is a fruitful arena for mind stretching and probably the only kind of social involvement that I can stand. A place to grow, and for the student and teacher to grow together. What was that descriptive phrase of a campus that I like so much ...... a *malleable microcosm of an existing and perfectible world*. Once the student grasps the thrill of being able to sense meaning on many levels at the same time, you can imagine the ecstasy as a teacher seeing that miraculous mental metamorphosis. To see it time and time again, and being able to mold it and relate to it. To perpetuate, perhaps, that creed we sought with such intensity, which is ageless and which becomes more precious with the passage of time. The demand to be human without illusion; naked without narcissism; loving without idealization; ethical without moral passion; restless without being classifiably neurotic; and political without fabrication."

Justin chuckled, almost knowing what might come next. "I feel like a straight man. But, I'll ask it anyway. What about beyond college?"

Willis returned the chuckle, being as relaxed as he could be knowing that, at least for the moment, this was a mind compatriot. He had been exposed to enough hostility not to recognize a congenial setting, and fervent to a high pitch about his ideals not to take advantage of the opportunity to pontificate. The disturbances beyond these walls seemed far away physically as well as emotionally. After all, this was no longer his struggle, no longer his command. He secretly regretted that the students had taken such an openly defiant stance. There had been little chance for negotiation and settlement. "The essay, *The Sense of Disrelationship*, in the anthology, *America the Unimagining*, describes the problem of reality more succinctly than I can: *When we systematize life we are saying that any other way outside of the system is impossible, for this and this will happen to you. We defend our systems by a stockade of consequences. And then somehow we forget that we created both the system and the consequences.* There are ways to live where no one can ever be blamed. Where no rule is ever made that cannot be unmade or changed, and where the exceptions make up the reality and the beauty of being human. In other words, as if I need other words for you, teachers should not be the agents for prevailing social moods, to inculcate more sequences of command and obey."

"Of course, the cynic would then ask what or how the student is to be prepared to meet or fit in with the outside world?"

"Paul Goodman, in his book, *Growing Up Absurd,* proclaims that there is no right education except growing up in a worthwhile world. He also formulated the concept of *inept social engineering* and that by working in rigid institutions with crooked purposes even an intelligent animal must make a moron of himself. Any attempt to deal with the system makes you a victim of it. Thus, the student has the benefit of having created a separate life, even if only on an intellectual level, at the university. Later on the two worlds collide. The one is the societal world that demands he bend to it in order to receive the creature comforts. The other lies in his own sphere of influence where he can be himself. Why, my friend, is the real world so unforgiving? We try to change young people, as they become adults. A conformist mold. Little wonder they balk at the sight of the molds. The group-on at Berkeley in 1964 and its aftermath was just the early manifestation of the actions on other college campuses, even the one here and now. It created the hippie movement itself, and it made little lasting impression on the culture conformists. But, its enthusiasm and vitality have never died. I dare say it never will. In his essay, *Students and the Velocity of History,* Arthur M. Schlessinger, Jr. claims that students, as everyone else, are caught up in the velocity of history. The determination to affirm the integrity of the private self against the enveloping structure and hypocrisies of organized society."

How could one not admire the intellect and the insight of such a person? To grapple time and time again with what most others consider the imponderables. This was a rare treat for Justin, even as the campus unrest swelled nearby. The significance of this encounter would stay with him for a long time to come. If only he could capture a small portion of the wisdom for his yet to be written book. "So, if I may draw on my own philosophical repertoire, as Elizabeth Mamers said so precisely in *The Vulnerable Generation,* it is better to light one candle than to sit and grumble in the darkness."

"Excuse the pun, but that is a wicked idea."

"Especially if the grand design is to burn the candle at both ends."

"You do realize, anyone overhearing this conversation would think we are both mad."

"It would serve them right. Besides, genius is a mental aberration. What I like to call Thinking Thoughts can appear outlandish to those not suffering from TT."

Before they parted, they compared the current student situation with the tempo of the circumstances from their era. Too many similarities, too many differences. Both were of the same opinion that the vantage point made the biggest difference. Whether you were them or us colored your principles and reinforced righteousness. Searching for a middle ground might be the biggest challenge and the largest failure.

When alone, Justin found himself once again in a personal transformation. It was extremely upsetting to realize that each major experience or strong personality crossing his path influenced his life in a more powerful way than his own mind set. It was as if he would conform to the influence as he perceived it, emerging in part as a new self. In such a state, how could he possibly be the master of his life's direction? Was he really that weak? Or, was he so unsure of himself that there was a need to mimic those he perceived to be strong or seemingly so sure of themselves. If he was in that caustic condition, how could he intrude on the lives of others? How could he pretend to guide young minds? How could he possibly sort out and resolve his romantic involvements? Of course, he might easily delude himself to think that he was practicing what he preached. Flexible enough to bend, open enough to greet new experiences, and honest enough to admit that he was not as yet a fully developed person. Of course, that does not do much for one's self-esteem. Self worth should never be underrated. Perhaps it is the key to self-control and self-direction.

He felt quite weary. He was having second thoughts about everything. All the good feelings generated by the seminars was lost in a twinge of guilt that much of the ideas he tossed out may have brought on much of the havoc. What he needed the most was to get away from it all, start fresh somewhere else, and to undertake something new. For a brief second, the haunting words of Dr. Mington echoed in his head. Yet, there was no way that he could abandon his commitments or turn his back on the situation that he may have been instrumental in creating or on the people that had entwined their lives with his. If only he could be perceptive enough to establish priorities. If only he could accomplish what needed to be done for him without hurting others. If only there were some easy answers. It seems that there never are.

TWENTY-TWO

How she arrived at such a critical juncture, she was at a loss to comprehend. Normally, she was in total control of her life and dictated the impact of persons and events on her well being. In fact, Kate Henderson had a reputation that she fostered. She was thought to be dictatorial, hard-boiled and intractable. It was not the composition for legend-creation, but it minimized the intrusions on her time and energy so that she could direct her destiny and achieve her goals. Now, as if the tables had been cruelly turned against her, she seemed to be at the mercy of an ill-defined romantic relationship. A double dilemma. A relationship slipping from her grasp, and now thrust right in the middle of an explosive campus situation.

Justin had been avoiding her. She so much wanted to share the amorous sensations that filled her being, vibrations that introduced new breadth and depth to her life's journey. Perceptive enough to know that he was wrestling with some inner turmoil, she had backed off so that he would not feel that she was smothering him. Hurt that he had not turned to her for comfort and counsel, the dilemma was to do nothing or risk an aggressive action. Just when she was readying herself to take some form of positive action, the college administration insisted that she be one of the three faculty members on a committee designated to hear the student demands and to be the intermediaries in any negotiating process.

The other two faculty members also had a radical filled past. Thomas Warville had been a teaching assistant at Berkeley. He had taken to the streets with the students and stripped of his coveted status. Not that he had minded such a sacrifice for a cause so just, but it had certainly unsettled his otherwise even-keeled plans and had become an obstacle in his career path until he had landed a teaching position at Blantyre. For the past five years he had taught an assortment of English classes, and had developed a good rapport with the students. He had distanced himself from his Berkeley days, and the gap had grown wider as he matured. Now, he felt that he was caught between and betwixt. Not an enviable posture, but this dynamic situation might just wind up to be the catalyst for his future entrenchment. Gordon Frantau was more of a scholarly radical. In-depth readings had tested his social mores, and at an early age he had totally rejected the dictates of a prudent society. His early writings, published in an array of anti-societal publications, were filled with inciting dogmas, half-baked ideas, and partially thought-out concepts. As he grew older, his position in direct opposition to staid principles was less inflamed and filled with greater thought and reason. He had been edging towards a middle ground, reaching as most maturing minds do that there are good and evil consternations on both sides of the problematic equation, and that compromise prompts practical and realistic action.

It was this trio that sat across the table in the Administration Building's largest conference room facing Ted Amherst and two of his most support-ive foot soldiers. Little did they know that it was a reluctant Ted Amherst, a man who had to face the brutal fact that one cannot necessarily break the shackles of the past or the present to be totally free to approach the future without restrictions.

As much as he had resigned himself in his deepest philosophical moments that he would not wind up doing what he did not fully believe in, Ted had found himself in a most tenuous position. Perhaps he had just been a leader for too long for him to throw off that beguiling mask without mon-umental effort, or for others to consider him in any other capacity. Without willing it, he had found himself in the middle of organizing and leading what could become the most massive demonstration on an American college cam-pus. A protest aimed at all of the targets of youth rebellion – university offi-cialdom, parental authoritarianism, war, poverty, perverted justice, social stultification, political mockery, economic double talk, and the entire false moral preaching inundating their daily lives. While it probably would not meet the 700 arrests made at the uprising at Columbia University in 1968, there were many followers willing to be arrested and to prepare and use incendiary devices with little regard to their personal safety and status. Even considering the new found discovery of his true self, he did have another reason for not being an excluded member. Consistent with his desire to show others through teaching, there was the hope that somehow he could direct this entire happening into a learning experience. A case of wishful thinking, no doubt. Then, of course, there was that certain allure of leadership that he could not quite relinquish. An exhilaration, the awe of idol worship, and the power of knowing, plotting and executing. Realistically, who could deny that he was in the stranglehold of coveted enthrallment? One way or another his private being was subordinated by an overpowering public role. As if it were a prearranged destiny, it was natural for him. Not all teaching occurs in the classroom. Learning is a constant.

What he needed more than anything else was a quiet time with Estelle. How he longed for that kind of respite! How little he had appreciated it when he had it. One of the more prominent human frailties – not knowing what one actually has until it is gone. He would lose himself in her arms, secure in that intimate contact from any ill conceived pressures. A vital repast, not having to think of causes or to say words to inspire. He so missed that, and he would gladly trade all of the drama and the forthcoming aftermath if he could recapture that bliss. Such was not to be. His immediate frame of reference was incompatible with that form of serenity.

He had even thought of further cultivating the discovered affinity with the young professor. Perhaps, even more than the bond between a man and a woman, there can be a special tie between two men or between two women. It is nearly impossible for a man and a woman to be total friends. Somewhere along that winding route the physical elements intrude, offsetting to a degree the full promise of friendship. Deep down he felt that he and Justin Post could become close friends. Especially now that he had found out that Estelle was seeing him. Instead of being jealous, he found that this served as an additional cohesive factor, a common force between them. Not that his vanity was showing, but Estelle would only have been attracted to Justin if there was the same characteristics that he had. The professor must have perceived in her the same qualities that he had sought. The natural intellectual similarities. Shared brotherhood. Intertwined humanity. A slogan for two. However, for all practical purposes, that too was not to be for the present time.

Kate tried to maintain an air of dignity, even though inside she was seething at the way the students had upset her life and routine. "As representatives of the faculty, we are here at your request to listen to what you have to say. You must understand that we are merely a reporting body. We have no authority to pass on the merits of your demands or to grant any concessions or favors. Is this understood?"

"Yes," Ted answered in an equally somber tone. "You should equally understand that the students have demanded this hearing in an attempt to cease the actions currently underway and planned for the future if the University will comply with what we offer. This is our only attempt to have a nonviolent resolution of the unfair conditions and treatment that the students suffer at the hands of the University. If the demands are not met in full, then the total responsibility must lay at the feet of the administrative body."

Kate straightened in her seat, pen in hand, poised to write down the forthcoming edict. She could not help but remember earlier days when her sentiments and beliefs might well have been on the other side of the table. Yet, the present situation did not seem to justify the reactions of the current students. There was no longer a war in Vietnam. A definite upsurge in the movement for civil rights and women's rights was apparent. Even the national organizations that had led the rebellions of the 60's had disbanded or changed their agendas. The underground press had all but disappeared. Like a vestige of the past, this haunting scene seemed out of place and out of step with the times.

Ted pulled a sheet of paper from the folder he was carrying. "You need not write this down, after reading from this sheet I will give it to you. There will then be no doubt or confusion about the realistic opportunities presented. "First and foremost, all students that have been arrested or otherwise held responsible for any damage shall be released and granted complete amnesty. There will be absolutely no penalty or recriminations against any student for participation in any demonstration or in show of support for the student actions. Second, a student-faculty-administration committee shall be formed. It will be comprised of four students, four faculty members, and two administration representatives. Its role will be to determine and implement University policy and programs, including all subject course offerings. Third, any cooperation between the University and the military in any potential war-related research and training is to be eliminated immediately, including discontinuance of the ROTC. Fourth, no faculty member shall be granted tenure. Faculty members will be retained solely on the basis of student evaluations of courses and seminars conducted. Fifth, there will be no interference or influence exerted in connection with any of the student newspapers or other publications. Sixth, any and all organizations and activities of the students will be encouraged and supported by the University and all of its officials. Seventh, the grading system will be changed immediately to a P for pass, E for excused, and N for not-passed.

Kate took the sheet of paper. "Hopefully, some discussion will follow on these points, although you might readily admit that they are one-sided. What I fail to comprehend is why it has all been necessary to disrupt everybody's lives before you have aired your feelings? Another puzzlement, why at this University, one of the most liberal in the country? Why couldn't you have just called a meeting like this before all of this, or formally submitted suggestions through designated channels? Bombings, sit-ins, class disruptions, fear in the community, extensive damage to school property, where is the payback? The pity of the public rests with the University, and you are branded as radicals in some circles and a laughing stock in others. I know I speak for all of us. Why couldn't you have tried to enlist our sympathies at an early stage instead of taking action into your own hands?"

Ted's response was swift and brutal. "Do you think we are so naïve to know that without such acts not only would there be no meetings but any student-generated ideas would have been dismissed as irrelevant and inconsequential? You of all people, those who have been through this in your own time, should know that actions speak louder than words. Of course, we regret the hurt and the damage, but this is our war and this is the one way to win it."

"How can you be so sure of that without giving peaceful resolution a chance first?" Kate shot back with a voice that even made her colleagues tremble.

Ted rose quickly to his feet. "End of discussion. See you on the battle-field or to sign an agreement to these terms."

Ted stormed out of the room, quickly followed by his cohorts. He knew that the theatrics were lost on the faculty members, but the word would spread to his disciples. He was confident that there was little choice but compliance from the other side, no margin of victory too large at this point.

Kate sighed, lost in despondent thoughts stretching far beyond this room. Most depressing of all was the eerie feeling that her involvement in this no win situation was not at an end.

TWENTY-THREE

With the college closed for the rest of the semester and the students banned and sent home for an early extended Christmas vacation, it suited Justin well. He actually started collecting notes for the book, and he hoped to use the time to good advantage. At this point, the book, or at least the thought of such a task, seemed to be the anchor in his life.

Estelle's kiss was still fresh on his lips. She had been so absorbed by the student situation that she happily left the status of their relationship stand as it was. His promise to visit her at home over the holiday was the signal she had sought. Fulfillment was attainable. She had left on a positive note, once again believing that her life would be righted and that brighter times lay just beyond the dark hills.

That left the situation with Kate and Rita to juggle. Both relationships were delicate. There was a great dependency by each of them on him. In the final analysis, it may not be the actual him but merely what he represented. A lifeline to cling to. An immovable object in a much too fluid surrounding.

Kate had stayed on at the campus. He had seen her last night before her departure home for the holiday. It did not portend to be a festive holiday. There were too many residuals from her recent involvement in the student uprising. When he arrived at her apartment for dinner, she looked pale and her embrace was tentative.

He peered deep into those magnetic eyes. "I am very sorry I have not been here for you more. It is not your doing. I know you have been more closely involved in this trouble than I have, and I do want you to know I am here to support you. I care about you more than my recent actions reveal."

She held him closer, stroked his cheek, and her lips expanded into that captivating smile. "I am pleased to hear that. I know you have your own pressures, and I also know that people need to share problems, perhaps even more than the good times. I did not want to be thrust into the confrontation with the students. Yet, it did bring a certain amount of clarity to my thinking. Maybe, it was just the sudden clash with my past. It has given me a new perspective on where I have been and where I am going. It is quite a revelation to find out that one's principles may not be as deeply entrenched as previously thought. It is also eye-opening to be on a different side than the one I was on for many years. I am still a so-called radical thinker and believer, but I think I have abandoned the concept of a straight course being the most effective. While you might get to the end sooner, there can be too much to discard along the way and less to savor at the goal."

After dinner, as they held each other close on the sofa, the haunting words of Emerson came to Justin's mind.

> *Life is a train of moods like a string of beads, and, as we pass through them, they prove to be many-coloured lenses which paint the world their own hue, and each shows only what has in its focus. From the mountain you see the mountain. We animate what we can, and we see only what we animate. Nature and books belong to the eyes that see them. It depends on the mood of the man, whether he shall see the sunset or the fine poem. There are always sunsets, and there is always genius, but only a few hours so serene that we can relish nature or criticism. The more or less depends on structure and temperament.*

> *When what you want doesn't happen, learn to want what does* [Arabia].
> *Fortune and misfortune dwell in the same courtyard* [Russia].

When they made love, it was gratifying to know that there was an affinity between them that grew stronger with the passing of time. For Kate, she was still uncertain of the true depth of his feelings for her, but she faced the relationship with a new resolve. She loved him more than she had ever loved any other man. That compounded her recent revelations. Yet, she no longer feared losing him. She had the moment, and was able to bask in this wonderful feeling. It gave her great inner confidence to know that she could feel this deeply, this completely. She also trusted him as she had never trusted any one else. She would leave the future to its own devices. By nourishing the moment, she was feeding her own being.

Rita was an entirely different predicament, with a troubling set of circumstances. Provocative clothing and an aggressive tactic were gradually wearing him down. Her youthful antics, merging sexual advances with child-like, playful mannerisms, were very reminiscent of the teasing that Rosalind had engaged in. Rita sent him a love letter, scribbled in crayon throughout a roll of toilet paper. Rosalind had done a similar creative ploy on a roll of paper that was designed for a cash register. Closely printed were assorted professions of love that took him hours to read. She had never told him how long it had taken to finish that opus, but the deed and fragments of its contents lingered in his emotional composite. He was so sure that unless he could place Rosalind properly in his past, he could never adequately handle any or all of his present involvements.

No road is so long in the whole land as from heart to head to hand
[Germany].
Walk fast and you catch misfortune, walk slowly and it catches you
[Russia].

In the quiet confines of his apartment, at long last he started the writing of the book. As yet untitled, to begin was necessary for there was much he had to say, much he had to let out. Designed to soothe the chaos of living for others, perhaps he might, through the same enterprise, steady his own life ship and set a definite course for its travel.

The book was started .

Principle #1. *It is better to listen than to speak.*

One of the more difficult things for young people to master is to listen carefully and fully to what is said, and then to think sufficiently before responding. Proverbs are rich in this philosophy. "A man has two ears and one mouth that he may hear much and speak little." [German proverb] "He who knows most speaks least." [Italian proverb] "Teeth placed before the tongue give good advice." [Italian proverb] "The tongue that is yielding, endures; the teeth which are stubborn, perish." [Chinese proverb]

Before he could transfer thoughts further, there was a knock at the door. Rita purposefully looked very much more mature than her tender years, and her smile was warm and inviting.

She pushed passed him into the room, throwing her coat on a chair on her way. "I am sorry. I could not stay away. I need to talk to you."

He motioned for her to sit on the sofa. She preferred to pace before him, so he sat down and watched her intently.

"I saved her life today, but I am not sure I did either one of us a favor. She was drunk, very drunk. She got into the tub to take a bath. When I heard the frantic splashing I rushed in and pulled her out. Her head was under the water. I can't go on like this."

"Rita, you must get professional help. Not only for yourself but for your mother as well. At your age, the responsibilities you are confronted by are too severe. I am not equipped to be of much help."

She took off her cardigan. Underneath was a leotard top, and the contours of her budding breasts were revealed in tempting ways. It was obvious that she had not worn a bra. There was no doubt in his mind that she had come here for more than one purpose. It was also going to be necessary for him to exercise some super control so that the situation would not get out of hand.

"Justin, can I stay here with you?"

"Rita, you know that is impossible. I want to help you, but this would accomplish nothing except to get us both into trouble."

"The here and now need not carry other difficulties."

"There is no way of being certain about that. I have come too far for this job to jeopardize it, not to mention problems with the law since you are under age."

"But, I love you. How else can I display it?" She sat down in his lap, and her youthful body was warm and inviting.

"Sometimes, love calls for great sacrifices. It is often displayed more in the not doing than in the doing. Besides, I do not think you love me. You love what I represent, an opportunity to get away from your home and your mother. Out there is a young man nearer your age who will gain your attention and affection."

"Can you deny that you want me?"

"Rita, you are on the verge of becoming a beautiful woman. No man in his right mind would not want you when that blossoming is complete. That does not necessarily mean that it should happen that way. We already have a wonderful relationship, a wholesomeness that would be compromised by a physical involvement."

She was quiet for a moment. Shrewdly, calculating that this must not be the right time to press on. "Alright, but can I have a hug?"

He clasped his arms around her, nearly intoxicated by the youthful fragrance. She felt his hardness beneath her, and sensed that victory would not be far off. "I accept this for now. But, I want you to be the first man to make love to me. If we have the closeness that you say we do, you will not deny me that request at some time soon."

Avoiding the momentary impulse seemed to be the most important objective. "We will see. The future is uncertain, people are unpredictable. You may well change your own mind."

"I doubt it. I really do."

She left, and he had the distinct impression that he had dodged a bullet. However, the gun was fully loaded. Other bullets would be aimed at him. Somehow, as much as he had wanted to control this kind of situation, there was the nagging feeling that he was playing right into her hands.

We each have our own story: how interesting our life's romance would be if we could but understand it ourselves. Those sage words of George Sand lingered in Justin's mind.

TWENTY-FOUR

Estelle paced nervously in the family room. The Christmas tree was especially festive this year, and her additional effort to make it so for Justin was evident. He was already overdue by several hours, and she was trying valiantly not to panic. Traffic and slick roads might certainly have delayed him, and she dared not to think of gruesome alternatives. The tenseness in the house was particularly unnerving. Her parents would undoubtedly be gracious, but the disapproval of this relationship permeated the holiday aura and the atmosphere was glum. They had talked seemingly without end, and even in the face of all of her exposition and pleading they remained unconvinced that the relationship was the transport for her life's quest. She begged them not to be judgmental. Just to give him a chance was her urgent request.

Mr. and Mrs. Winslow did not appreciate how this man had manipulated and monopolized their daughter's emotions and outlook. They could not grasp the change in her attitude and demeanor. A few months ago she was an exuberant youth swept up in the adventure of learning and growing. Now, she was intransigent and fixated on one person. Experience tainted their intuition about this man who had robbed her of her youth. They did not want their only child to have her promise for career and achievement cut short. Her sensitivity and intellect could take her a long way on life's journey so long as she did not settle for some early restriction. A serious relationship, particularly with one who was more advanced in years and experience, would be nothing less than a confinement. Justin Post was a serious threat to her well being and to their expectations. It mattered not that her face had a glow when she spoke of him. Her assertion that two could well travel as far if not farther along the paths of achievement fell on deaf ears.

Under the circumstances, when Justin agreed to come for dinner one day only, Estelle readily agreed although she had hoped to have a prolonged family assimilation. That was now a fading hope. He was already late for the limited time that might be available to win over the brooding doubts of the family. Estelle was nervous, not so much for the ensuing events as much as for the seemingly inevitable dilemma for a choice between devotions. If it came to such a decision, it was already made. Consequences were of little concern when her mission was at stake.

As Justin drove carefully through the mix of precipitation, numerous thoughts and visions further clouded his outlook. Too many demands splintering his attention. Too many uncertainties with his actual desired role in the midst of fast moving events.

He put his hand up to his nose. It felt cold. The car's heater did an ample job of adding warmth to the small confines of the automobile and to defrost the windows. His nose had often shown signs of succumbing to the cold before other parts of his body. In fact, Rosalind had used that attribute as an easy vehicle to tease him. When they would kiss and the tip of his nose would graze her cheek, her eyes would spring open and a faint giggle would form in the back of her throat. As a surprise gift, she knitted him a nosewarmer. A gray woolen cap that had long ends that tied behind his head. Frightful to behold, but certainly clever and utilitarian. Just one of many creative outpourings of her love. He had let all of that go. Such a huge regret did not make his present plight any easier to work out.

A bit later, standing before Estelle's door, the wet snow fell upon his head and landed full on his face. So reminiscent of a poignant event of the distant past. He was holding Rosalind in his arms on a warm evening and the rain seemed cool against their enflamed bodies. The water rolled down their cheeks and dampened the joined lips. The outside world was far removed from their isolated existence, and it mattered not who saw them or who may have disapproved of the shocking behavior. For that moment, then and there, they were in love as much any two people might be. Looking back on that now, he failed to recognize and appreciate that spellbinding moment as an indication of the lasting sensation of true devotion. A kiss full of the magical combination of strength and tenderness. Wild, ecstatic, and uncontrollable. An embrace of great promise. Yet for him and because of him, a strength sapped by disuse, a tenderness lost in a tomorrow and a bright promise unfulfilled. The glory of another day. The disappointments of today.

Estelle came rushing to the door when the bell sounded. She flung open the door and smothered him with kisses before he could cross the threshold. Youthful vibrancy as a manifestation of passionate caring. The earnest emotion was uncontrollable. He drew a deep breath and entered another phase of his ever restricting life.

The dinner was an ordeal for all of them. Tension was the main course. Little conversation was offered, and, while polite, there was no mistaking Mr. and Mrs. Winslow's lack of appreciation for this stranger in their lives. They had protected and nurtured their little girl from birth, and this situation was a serious threat to the bonds so carefully secured over the years. Perhaps Estelle's biggest disappointment was the obvious failure on their part to see any of this through her eyes. It was not her intent, nor the inevitable outcome, that the family would be set apart. On at least one level she was presenting an opportunity to expand the family with the addition of a person who could be a wonderful "son" if they gave him that chance. Sure, she had not contemplated at this stage of her life that she would have met that special person with whom she wanted to spend the rest of her life. But, it had happened, and not only was it enhancing this aspect of her growth, but also supplying the solace and fortitude for what lay beyond. Why, oh why, couldn't they see that?

"Justin," Mr. Winslow spoke in a steady and somber voice, "I hear that you are a successful author?"

Justin responded guardedly, "Success is a measured term. I was fortunate enough that my talents were afforded an opportunity to be put to use after I was in the right place at a wrong time. Success was not the object then, or is it now."

"I meant successful in the sense of financial reward."

"It has not brought me riches. It has led to a comfortable situation, and has given me the wherewithal to pursue the next step."

"What is that?"

"I have started on a new book. New in the sense of another undertaking, but it is really merely an outgrowth of the first one. I am hoping that its societal impact will be far greater. Your wonderful daughter has in many ways been the catalyst for this endeavor."

"Is there financial security in being an author?"

"The money is secondary. I feel I have a chance to assist young people to find purpose and meaning in life. I intend it to be motivational."

"Do you mean to help them find a job?"

"A job can certainly be a part of the equation. It is more in the direction of keying in on confidence building and seeking personal serenity. To know that the possibility that a niche exists in the scheme of humanity for each person to discover and take pleasure in."

"I can see why you are a teacher. Ideas for the classroom. I believe more in practicality. The actual day-to-day struggle of people in the marketplace. This other stuff is more philosophical, perhaps to prod and expand the mind but of little value in providing for a family."

"Why don't you tell me what is really troubling you? Is it your concern that I do not have your daughter's best interests at heart? Despite the difference in our ages and our posture along life's curve, I assure you that I am not in her life to hurt her or misguide her. I am not going to control her and dictate her choices. She is a very mature woman, with deep and abiding feelings. She is more than capable of knowing what she is doing and why she is doing it. You have done a marvelous job of raising her. Her sense of family and warm personal contact is a product of the principles and sentiment you have instilled in her."

"You speak as if that job has already been completed. Our concern is that we do not want her to be suffocated. She has so much to experience, so many new people to meet and new events to participate in. To be candid, we think a serious relationship is premature, far too early for her. You may be ready, but she has a lot of growing to do."

He wanted to convince them that they had not taken a good look at her.

That they had failed to recognize that she is an adult, fully able to comprehend her actions and their consequences. He was astute enough to know that this was an emotional conversation, and that intellect would not save it. There would be no dissuading them of their belief, and further attempts might solidify their posture and make things more difficult for Estelle. So, he let the conversation rest even if it had given them the false impression that they were so right that there was no adequate response. Perhaps, upon reflection, it might be best at this juncture that they see him as an object of Estelle's infatuation that will fade away with time and diversion.

They only had a brief moment alone before he left. Totally unsatisfying if a fulfillment of a love contract was desired. Yet, it placated her to know that he had cared enough to be there and to endure the unpleasant atmosphere. No matter how abbreviated his embrace was, it was soothing and reinforcing. It was enough to fortify her, to set her mind on a firm future together. It was of little consequence even if the rest of the world disapproved of their match. Her life could only now be thought of in terms of *theirs* and a future only in the conceptual framework of *ours*. The meaningful words of DeStael filtered through her mind. *Love is the emblem of eternity; it confounds all notion of time: effaces all memory of a beginning, all fears of an end.*

As Justin drove away, adding the mileage between them, he was inwardly tormented. The same old dilemma in a slightly different variation. The love he had thrown away in the past imbued this present love with a sense of unreality. An outsider, privileged only to see the inner workings and powerless to affect actions or results. Not the kind of situation he needed or wanted. Not the position he had ever envisioned for what he once thought was a well-conceived plan.

TWENTY-FIVE

The school was closed for the rest of the semester. The students were advised not to return but would be welcome for a delayed opening for the Spring semester. Two of the smaller buildings had been damaged extensively. The barren campus attested to the hollowness of the events that had occurred. Any future was held in abeyance.

Justin read the letter three times to dispel the utter disbelief as to its contents. He had been dismissed – fired. It had supposedly been reported to the reigning officials that he had fomented the uprising. His classroom urgings for carrying out anarchist upheavals had helped to incite the students to violent behavior. His seminar had allegedly been the kindling for the full conflagration Blantyre experienced. It seemed clear that the University and the students sought a scapegoat to explain the imponderable. Someone to blame. A focal point of refutation so that each side might be exonerated on the surface and enable them to begin anew.

An astute observation by Emerson enabled him to regain perspective. *Life is a series of surprises. We do not guess today the mood, the pleasure, the power of tomorrow, when we are building up our being.*

There was an initial hurt, a burning disappointment of injustice directed at him. Then, the more he thought about it, some positive element came to the fore. It might very well be an opportunity. It represented a built-in excuse to side-step the intractable romantic involvements, and propel him on the most practical course for writing the book. He needed to retreat to a quiet haven where he could work without interruption and distraction. His personal reason for being at Blantyre had been blunted by a series of failures. His own life needed greater attention and organization. Most important of all, he had yet to break the shackles of living in a memory.

Every future is not far away [Arabia].

He felt no allegiance to the University, and its stance was weak and probably designed to placate the public. The students, as with all young people, attempted to make mature decisions without having the experience and wisdom that such decisions demand. He had failed himself by letting them down. He had wanted to sow the seeds of their discontent in an inward direction rather than outwardly. Their true unrest was with their inner turmoil to better a world in the face of an apathetic adult block. The University was merely a symbol, convenient to strike out against. He had hoped that the seminar might soothe the anger and redirect the discontent. If he had not reached a degree of success there, with all of the effort he had put into it, then how might he succeed in any way with the book? The seminar did only advance portions of discourse, without continuity and conclusion.

The greater the insight the greater the fore sight [Germany].

The book, in its entirety, hopefully would provide enough insight and adequate direction for even a few of these impounded souls. The book certainly would be a catharsis for him. There were many loose ends demanding attention. Many explanations, much hurt. Time, a tough taskmaster, would render the final judgment of his success.

First resolve what must be done; solutions will then be evident [China].

He should have guessed that the first person to know about this turn of events would be the one who probably precipitated it. When he opened the door to the fervent knocking, he was not totally surprised to see Ted Amherst standing there. The young radical pushed passed him into the room.

There was no doubt that Ted was agitated. Not only had the school not accepted their demands, but by isolating some of the weaker students, it had been determined that there was not enough cohesion behind the actions to support a firm position. Names were uttered, fears expressed, and the force splintered. Parental involvement had even negated some of the staunchest basic assertions. In fact, as irony would have it, Ted stood nearly alone in the face of the administrative onslaught even though he no longer considered himself the students' leader.

Ted's tone matched his heightened state of emotion. "I had no idea this would happen. Believe me."

"How did it happen?"

"A mixed-up plan. A goal gone crazy. What I looked on as an intellectual exercise. They asked me to put in writing the whole thing.....why we did it, what we were really after, and did we think we accomplished anything."

"And, instead of being fully intellectual, you let some emotional energy emphasize your personal posture instead of keeping it as general as possible."

"How did you know that?"

"Another sort of intellectual exercise. Because, my young friend, I dare say I would have reacted the same way. You are in too deep to admit you are wrong. The action was taken, fully planned that way or not, and in an attempt to rationalize it there is the tendency to ward off personal fault when feasible."

"And," his shoulders slumped as he sat down on the floor, "when all is said and done, I know that we are worse off now than we were before. We have breached the physical sanctity of the institution, the significance of which we worship. We have lost our credibility. To make it even worse, I have lost my bearings. My resolve is crushed. Does it make any sense at all?"

"Well, you cannot undo what has been done. But, there are many lessons to be learned here, some very personal to you. Instead of concentrating on where you went wrong, look ahead and firm up your future role in trying to make up for any wrongs committed, for achieving what's right in the most reasonable way for success. I would think the most valuable lesson you can take from all of this is that there are times, often the difficult times, when you must lose yourself before you can find yourself."

Ted dropped his gaze to the floor. His voice was now sedate, almost forlorn. "Without you here to emulate, I will be swallowed up."

Justin sat beside him on the floor and put his arm around the broad shoulders. "I doubt that. You rose to a position of leadership because that was what you deemed was needed of you. On that same basis, you can and will emerge in a part of life's play that you set for yourself. Just make sure that the path is well defined and that you are sure where you want to wind up. Confidence in yourself is the first prerequisite. You really need no one else to guide you."

"You sure are a confidence-builder."

"I don't believe it is so. I just seem to have an inherent talent of seeing clear paths for others. It is a gift, perhaps. My problem is applying it to myself."

"You certainly turned me around 180 degrees. I am indebted to you."

"No, don't let yourself feel that way. Some people need to see themselves first in others before they can find themselves. Your case, plain and simple."

Ted rose to his feet. "Again, I am really sorry it turned out this way for you, as well as for me."

"Think of it not as an ending but as a turning point. Consider it your turn for your efforts for you."

The two men shook hands, knowing that there was a strong bond between them. Probably they would never cross paths again, but each had influenced the other. That kind of contribution to development is carried forward for a lifetime.

Lessons can be learned from all experiences. In fact, the lessons themselves are the bridges between experiences.

To go beyond is as bad as to fall short [China].

Return to old watering holes for more than water; friends and dreams are there to meet you [Africa].

The situation with Kate would not be so easily resolved. He needed to approach it now, while simple truths would be the most reasonable, believable and tolerable.

He went to the telephone and dialed Kate's number. The responding voice was soft and resonant.

"Hello, Kate," he managed to utter.

"Well, I thought you had fallen off the end of the Earth."

"That would have been too easy."

"Someone sounds despondent."

"That and more."

"Too pressured to come over for some hot chocolate?"

"I'll be there in fifteen minutes."

Kate had been despondent herself. She still could not shake off the recent events with the students, especially her inept involvement. Not sure whether she had ever really had him, she had felt that Justin was gradually slipping away. Her feeble attempts at intellectual matters were frustrating and unproductive. For the first time in a very long chunk of her life she seemed to be drifting, and there appeared to be no safe shore for her to pull over to. Self-pity was a luxury for others, not for her.

When Justin arrived, one look told her that there was more at stake than a fleeting unhappy moment. The gist of a poem by Alice Duer Miller came to mind. Bad news is not necessarily broken by a kind tactful word, but its message often is preceded by a person's bearing, the way a breath may be drawn, or the look in the eye. All so that the heart despairs before the ears hear.

She was not surprised that the University had found a scapegoat. Yet, it had to be just a temporary reprieve. Too many seething problems existed, and even the faculty was restless. She could deal with this surface inequity. Strangely, it left her with a renewed sense of strength, and she was genuine in her attempt to bolster his spirits. After all, he had turned to her for just this kind of solace. So, she helped him focus on the opportunities that may have been forced on him, and encouraged him to take full advantage of them.

Warm conversation carried them through an hour, and each knew that their physical relationship had come to an end. It was replaced with a deep sense of commitment that two intellectuals can share who have similar aspirations. Justin would never stop marveling over this warm and fervent woman, so strong, so deep.   She had given him so much more than he had given her.

For Kate, the form was unpredictable, but the surprise was not really a surprise.   She had actually steeled herself for what she had sensed was inevitable.   Justin's sagging interest and evident distancing of himself had portended an exit from her life.   She found herself comfortably resigned to a return to the period when she needed no one else to sail through life's ocean.   It was a course she may not have wanted, but it was a familiar one. Justin had not made any promises or offered any great expectation.   Rather, he had captured a moment, shared it with her, and supplied a refreshing interlude in an otherwise stagnant life.   She was a willing participant, and its significance would endure.   She knew she could love deeply.   The disappointment was with the facts and not with herself or with Justin.   It turned out not to be as painful as she had anticipated.

TWENTY-SIX

A coating of new fallen snow clung to every branch and vegetative appendage. No other cars were on the road, and in the darkness of the night the snow seemed to exude a light of its own. A symbol to represent a fresh beginning, or merely a blanket hiding imperfections beneath it? For a writer, too many ordinary occurrences lurking as symbols. Too many chances; too many choices. No respite from mind extension in probing ideas. Too many thoughts intertwined, intermingled. Apparently no beginning, no end, and only confusion obliterating all attempts at demarcation.

As the car pulled up in front of her house, Rita was waiting for him outside. Her breath sent vapors into the chilled night air. Her coat was much too flimsy for the low temperature. She slid in next to him and he turned the car's heater to high.

She sat close to him as they drove off, her hand resting lightly on his thigh. They did not speak until he pulled the car into a desolate area. He left the motor running so that the heat would continue to warm the interior.

Justin turned to her, in full admiration of the budding innocence sculptured so finely in that beautiful, youthful face. "I have some difficult news to break to you."

Her smile was wide, and her hand patted his thigh. A most suggestive motion at another time, in another setting. "I already know."

"How did you find out?"

"You forget. This is a small town. Few things happen that aren't spread rapidly. A faculty wife couldn't wait to tell my mother, and she blurted it out to me."

"Of course, that is only half of the news."

Her eyes shifted to the floor and he sensed her body stiffen. "And you are leaving," her voice raising to a high pitch, "Running away, just as my father did."

"I don't look at it as running away. There is nothing here I wish to escape from, other than a hurtful personal injustice. Rather, I am simply shifting location. I will be going to a place where I can work on my book without distractions."

"And, I am a distraction." Her voice trailed off in a somber note depicting her rejection.

Rita had it all planned. She was going to put him on the defensive and make him feel guilty about leaving her. To take out on him all of the rage she felt towards her father for abandoning the family. It was a curse, however, that she had read so many books. Experiencing through literature the full range of human capabilities, including excessive cruelty and evil intent. That exposure left her with a great deal to compare actual behavior to. So, even after plotting each intricate detail of the deflation of his spirit and will, she could not react with pure emotion. Justin was not her father. In fact, he had not left her in her time of need. He had been there for her to lean on when the need bordered on desperation. His advice had been comforting. His presence had bolstered her protective role with her mother, as well as the nurturing one for herself. It had given her the strength and confidence to hold the thin fragments of the remaining family on a common course. In the brief time that she had become close to him, she had matured because a steady hand was held out for her to take a hold of when her balance was at risk. She was able to recognize, respect, and accept the fact that he had a need of his own and that that need did not include her. She had even gone one step beyond that. There were asserting needs of her own, and those did not include him. At various interludes of life, needs come and go. The truly fortunate people can rightfully tell when one is over and a new one has taken its place. They then can change with it.

Nothing dries sooner than a tear [Germany].

Justin saw the far-off look in her eyes, sensing that she was engaged in an inner conflict. He was prepared for an onslaught. He just did not want the hurt to be devastating and permanent.

She turned to him, lifting her hand off of his leg. "I did not want to make it easy for you. I have needed you so much, and was even willing to give you my greatest gift.....my virginity. But, you have already done so very much for me. I can't deny that. I cannot be ungrateful, as much as I might want to stop you, and to keep you here. I do understand that I cannot control you. I just want you to know that in some way, a way that I am at a loss to express in words, I will always need you."

"That is heartening to know. Your need, as you will become more aware of, is what I represent for you. Someone who genuinely cares about you. Someone who notices and takes pride in what you accomplish. Someone who is cognizant of, and will listen to the expressions of what you feel, what you think, and what you dream. The wonderful qualities of you."

Those poignant words of Colonel Robert G. Ingersoll came gently to his mind. *I have a little short creed of my own, not very hard to understand, that has in it no contradictions, and it is this: Happiness is the only good. The time to be happy is now. The place to be happy is here. The way to be happy is to make others so.*

Justin grasped her dainty hand. "While I may be some distance away, we will remain close somehow."

"I truly hope so."

"You may not realize this, and I do not want to swell your head so that none of your winter hats will fit properly, but you have given me a great deal."

"Like what?"

"You have provided a counter balance for the tense academic environment. The most important thing is that you have given me a sense of family. You are as a sister that I never had. A home that welcomed my every arrival. An unreserved acceptance of each attempt I made to guide you. A youthful vitality that has restored my faith in people."

"I have done all that?"

"Yes, you have. You are already a woman, and quite a woman at that!"

"Imagine what I could have done if I had actually tried to be helpful. I think you give me much too much credit, but I'll not refuse it. I want you to remember me as the one who gave you all of that." She bent over towards him and kissed him lightly on the cheek. "Now, please take me for some hot chocolate. I need to have some warmth in my belly to match the glow in my heart."

The worst things in life are: To be in bed and sleep not, To want for one who comes not, To try and please and please not [Arabia].

Later, after he had dropped her off at the house, and they had hugged their farewells, Justin could bask in the total amazement of this young woman. This was one youngster he really did not have to be concerned about. Responsibility and awareness had given her a distinct advantage in meeting and mastering life's thorniest problems. While her family situation had been extremely painful, it had supplied her with an insight into a wide array of human behavior. At the same time, it enabled her to look outward with a keen perception of the happenings in which she was involved as well as to the persons who had varying degrees of influence on her future. In turn, she was able to garner whatever means that were necessary under the circumstances to meet an onslaught. To a small degree, he was envious. If only he could do as well. He was not even able to pretend he could. If he could not fool himself, there was little doubt that he could not come across that way to others.

TWENTY-SEVEN

Justin gazed through the wide picture windows of the sunroom at the gleaming river winding its way through the valley. The scene was artfully framed by the last vestiges of autumn color on the trees of the mountains descending down to the valley. He could scarcely believe that it was almost a year since he had left Blantyre. The small house seemed to be out on a cliff overlooking the river. It was a writer's panacea. The bright, cheerful sunroom, with its dazzling view, was restful, energizing, and inspiring, all at the same time. It beckoned him to write, and write he did. Passion tinged his words, and endless profound thoughts exuded from the typewriter. The book was almost finished. His personal transformation was complete. His entire being was at peace.

For awhile, he thought he had accomplished little at Blantyre. When it all settled into his mind, he had satisfied his reasons for being there. The seeds had been planted during the brief time that he was there – the struggle of the students, the ideas exchanged, the close relationships experienced. All making their way to fruition in the torrid writing. The book served as the final valve for the escape of all of the pent-up guilt and inner turmoil, so that he might face events and people with ease and confidence. While he still thought of Rosalind, the drifting into the past was becoming fewer and farther between. The emphasis had been altered. That past represented a monumental lesson for him. Love cannot be put at jeopardy, and one must never give up goodness once one has obtained it.

His thoughts were interrupted by a gentle touch on his shoulder and a soft kiss on his neck. He grasped Estelle's hand just before she spoke light-heartedly, "I thought you had given up on dream breaks."

"Even if I dream of you?"

"A very good response, my loving professor."

He pulled her around onto his lap and they kissed with an intensity that neither seemed to tire of. They had been married for nine months, and the honeymoon was on-going. A reaffirmation that a second love can be as poignant as a first one.

Over the protestations of her parents, Justin had headed straight for her home after he had packed the car. After a hasty blood test, they were married late that evening by a Justice of the Peace who had to pull two witnesses out from a laundromat next door. From there they started on life's adventure together, confident that they had made the right decision.

For Estelle, there was never any doubt. This man was her destiny, and the fulfillment of her being. She cherished this love house that they had found together. She was able to enroll and retake her senior year in a small college nearby. She basked in the new friends they made in the local writer/artist colony, where ideas were exchanged without hesitation or restriction. Wit often ran rampant, and she laughed more than she could ever remember. She had been able to write a weekly article for the local newspaper, and had become involved with the burgeoning movement to save the environment. They hiked, explored new places to visit or dine, and participated in all of the local historical and cultural events that surrounded them. She savored every word that he wrote, and served as a sounding board for his many and diverse thought patterns. All the time marveling that such a deep and caring man could love her as she wanted and needed to be loved. In May, when she would graduate, they planned to start a family. This, too, appeared as the natural culmination of this loving union. Even her parents warmed up to Justin, and they had visited them twice. They were pleased she was finishing school, and could not refute her happiness and obvious feeling of contentment. They could see how good he was to her and for her, and that erased many of the earlier apprehensions.

"I am about to finish the last chapter," he said with a tinge of sadness.

"Good. There will be even more time for you to love me."

"You mean before I start my new book."

"Only if it is the love story about us."

"Just what I had in mind."

"With pictures?"

"A few of me."

"Maybe, I better write this one."

"You already have."

Reluctantly, she pulled away from his lap, and smiled that captivating smile. "Please finish so we can start."

"Start what?"

"Making the movie of our love story."

"I guess I'll play me. Maybe I can get Natalie Wood to play you."

"Not a chance, Mister. I am in the contract."

"O.K. I'll suffer through it."

He watched her as she moved gracefully to the next room. His heart was brimming over. Little wonder the ideas flowered in his mind. He no longer had to dream.

Returning to the typewriter, the closing of the book spilled out on to the paper.

Physical deprivation and hardship are relatively unknown to most American youths. However, as discussed at length here, they know and must endure a mental agony no less debilitating. The inner torment in the youthful spirit. Tension can be filled with pain and uncertainty so as to leave any accomplishment as nebulous as its foundation. The final accounting perhaps never to be fully known or understood. Yet, not to be undone, ever.

Young people are a brooding lot. Questions loaded upon questions, doubts heaped upon doubts, and in the end they wind up to be their own severest critics. Controversy over exactly what to consider, or even when to begin deliberations. Analyses and techniques encumbered by varying interpretations of facts and impressions, leading to a potentially vast array of conclu-

sions. The subjective and objective so intertwined that the whole rarely appears in the same form twice. The desire to know. The incapacity to do something about it. The powerlessness to distinguish hesitation as being from strength or weakness. The consuming need to be accepted by others. The crux of it all – the underlying theme accentuated by the seemingly unfulfillable demands made by others and society as a whole, sharpened by personal expectations, muddled by countless stories and partially understood observations of the accomplishments by others, and often torn apart by conflicting and unmanageable inner desires. The propounded questions of the often overwhelming search for identity. Who am I? Where am I headed to? Who cares where, how or when I go? And, if I ever get there, how will I know it? Then, what do I do?

Overshadowing the entire complex picture is the near obsession to be grown-up. To be looked upon, called, and treated as an adult. The tragic fact that few of us reap the benefits and enjoyments of the growing years, and often look back later with regret. George Metsky, in his article The Ideology of Failure *that appeared in the Berkeley Barb, November 18, 1966, described it succinctly. "From the time we begin to call our childhood our past we seek to regain its simplicity."*

We have too long been counseled into merely recognizing successes or misfortunes, internal and external, to see that many variations are possible. Neither is an absolute, and each should properly be gauged by degrees. Compounding the equation is the perhaps illogical observation that one person's success might very well be another's failure. For good and evil, the causes are to be found in the mirror.

To explain any of it outright, so that a particular event or feeling retains any meaning for the given moment or the future depends not only on the unknown inner responses of the participant but also on that of the explainer. Cosmic vastness can easily separate these two truth seekers. A very difficult endeavor, and maybe even a cruel one to even undertake. Fault so easily becomes experience, and explanation too easily becomes acceptance. The outspoken idea becomes the preferred notion. Ritual becomes practice, following becomes habit, and living becomes mere existence. To doubt becomes the equivalent of weakness or oddity. To experiment appears radical or deviant, and to reach out brings further confusion and anxiety. Moods and temperament become the vessels of inquiry, leading to conflicting or confusing realms of belief. Raising, full circle, the same dilemma in a different mode. What is reality? Where does it begin and end? Does something less or different take over? Is self-recognition merely a personal answer to that imponderable? Is that the way it is supposed to be? The ultimate conflict. The wish to be different, the need to be the same. So much to know, to find out about. So few places one is welcome at and able to explore unimpeded. So little patience to contemplate what is seen, read and heard. Societal cracks turned into personal chasms.

A large part of the personal issue confronting us all is whether self-fulfillment requires the building of an individual philosophy rather than adopting one already established and espoused. Regrettably, some never even get to the point of acknowledgment that such a choice is possible. For the rest of us, perhaps it is simply the need to capture experience to make it understandable and productive. Does one gain insight into what life is about by being told what it is, or what one imagines it to be?

At some point, many of us arrive at the ultimate introspection of deciding what paths to transverse and in what direction to travel. The inevitable questions then emerge. Whether to arrive at goals is as important as having them in the first place? Whether the feeling good about oneself inures in the doing or the wanting to do? How can you find yourself? How can you be yourself? Is it all self-delusion? Is the armor of illusion penetrable? A flotilla of personal vanity looking for the perennial safe harbor. A predilection of self-esteem or self-destruction?

Do any of us know the difference? And, if we did, what would we do about it?

The biggest job any individual has is to make life one's own. But, what sort of guidance or training does one receive? Told to prepare for a job so as not to go hungry is overly simplistic. The world is full of material things, and too often the accumulation and possession of those items is equated with happiness. One is not told or encouraged to believe that there is another need brewing within. Can one truly be satisfied with a life that is a replica of countless others? Is being a rubber stamp automaton the kind of being that one needs to be or deserves to be? What are the true contours of human fulfillment? Where can one find the answers and who will assist in posing the right questions and pointing out the possible directions for external and internal travels? It may be frustrating and depressing to dwell on this, but not to do so is to be submerged in the motionless pool of mental stagnation.

There is more to being an individual than merely having a different name or an unusual face. There is more to it than conforming to an assigned role in the life play. The scope of the mind's direction and expanse is inviting. There is some mysterious force within and between people that make each of us uniquely human. Let it soar on the majestic wings of belief and action!

Our most valuable resource is the human spirit, and an upheaval, such as youthful rebellion, reaffirms such as being alive and well. Without it there is nothing but the shallows of the passing of time, memorializing only the deeds of the past. It can represent a positive statement that each of us does not have to accept things as they are.

When all is said and done, even though it is a world we never made, that does not mean we have to accept it as it is. We can work with and for others to change it. Perhaps, not completely or all at once, but it can be done. A Japanese proverb conjures up an appropriate image:

Even a mountain can be worn away by the tread of many feet.

There is also the possibility of making a special place within it just for ourselves. A warm, inviting niche to allow us to think without limitations, to feel without inhibitions, to exist without criticism or rebuke by others. A space reserved for the inner self to rise to the surface and to elevate to a plateau from which all can be observed and understood without outside influences. A safe, secure and congenial mental and emotional fortress. A place called home.

Printed in the United States
4616